Gray

By Rachel Karns

ISBN-13: 978-0615476674
ISBN-10: 0615476678

For Erik

Preface: The Stranger

Isolation was meant to heal him. And it did. He was happy, or at least at peace, doing what he felt he was born to do in the wild. For the last three years, Peter Delano was a stranger to everyone he met, and that felt safe. Life consisted of only himself and the wolves and an occasional short stay in Wallace.

Wallace was an unrealistically antiquated mining town nestled at the base of the protruding Silver Mountains. Not quite a ghost town but nearly abandoned, just the way he liked it. He kept an apartment here, just to shower, collect mail, restock supply, and to store the one modern convenience that necessitated his work: his laptop. All his time in the mountains was not in vain. He was working via a government grant, tracking the reintroduction of gray wolves in the North Idaho Panhandle, studying their pack mentality in the Silver Valley, their migration patterns through the Clearwater National Forest, their feeding habits and potential and already-realized hazards. It was a risky move to bring back a predator. Can nature be controlled, calculated, predicted? His job was to determine that and to report statistical data on a quarterly basis to the Idaho Fish and Game. The government left him alone with his wolves, paid for what he called his base-camp apartment, paid all his bills, and his frugality was his bonus. He wasn't going to be a burden on anyone.

Three years have passed since he last had any meaningful contact with another human being. Maya, the one he trusted with everything, the beautiful Maya whom he envisioned growing old with, left him nearly three years ago to the day. She loved the wolves and supported his research, yet she was social. Love wasn't enough--for her.

Maya met a pilot online, by accident she swore. In her attempt to feel connected, she joined a social network which led her back to some old friends and their acquaintances. Realizing how much more exciting everyone else's lives seemed, she kissed Peter goodbye, pleaded for forgiveness, and caught the first flight to Chicago, free of charge as she met her online "friend" at the terminal, dressed in pressed blue and white. Peter hated the laptop for its role in tearing them apart and would have loved to throw it off a cliff. Yet the laptop was his avenue to communicate his research to the IFG, and it was the avenue in which a new woman came into his life.

Eco-singles was a site meant for nature-loving singles, but he found it to be a general meat market of phonies who had a superficial passion for nature. He was just browsing--well, truthfully, he was hoping to find Maya's profile, hoping that she was miserable and too embarrassed to admit her mistake of leaving him. She wasn't there. Peter found himself quickly addicted, searching for Maya, and along the way found himself following the posts of another woman, possibly half as cynical as he was, and their banter was a distraction, if not slightly entertaining. Their jabs back and forth began a six-month fencing match.

She wanted to meet him. After months of flirty pessimism, she called his bluff. "I think you're scared." His ego got the better of him, and he agreed to meet her at Beverly's Lounge for drinks and live music, three towns away. If it didn't work out, there would be no chance of running into her in Wallace.

Just off the mountain, his clothes were disgusting. No time to hit the laundromat. He would have to settle for the only clean pair of jeans he owned and a brown, musty tee shirt he found in the bottom of his single dresser. Brute would cover that--and a shower--and a shave. He looked like a mountain man, not bothering with personal hygiene when he was in the mountains. Peter stared at his scrappy visage in the mirror. Nothing like scaring a woman on a first date than realizing she's been conversing with the Unabomber. Maybe he would keep the beard; the date would most certainly end quickly. He knew the date was destined for failure, because she wasn't Maya. Cynicism was seeping in, again. Of course he would shave, if he had any shaving cream. Or soap. Geez, he was completely hopeless.

Peter grabbed five dollars out of the cash can he stored in the kitchen cupboard and stuffed it in his filthy, tattered pants pocket. He left his apartment unlocked, quickly walking down to the Wallace Five & Dime in search of soap and shaving cream. The most he could give her would be the effort to smell clean, unlike his wet, wooly socks. That's about all he could promise.

Distracted with fighting his inner urge to stay home and avoid feelings that he had worked so hard to suppress, along with realizing that it was three minutes before six o'clock, when the Five &

Dime closed, he bolted into the two-lane street. There's no such thing as traffic in Wallace, usually.

No screech was heard on Cedar Street, because the driver of the car traveling that night didn't have time to consider braking in time. Shattered glass, mangled metal, blood, lots of blood. The only proof that the driver attempted to avoid hitting the pedestrian was the shattered asphalt bench that he swerved into, with shredded rubber leading to it. Ironically, the car dented the plaque that used to hang on the bench, reading *In Memory of so and so.*

Chapter One: Maggie

I first heard about the accident on the drive home from the airport. The top-of-the-hour news announced on the radio:

> "They are calling him John Doe. A man in Wallace was struck by a pizza delivery driver and has been in a coma since Saturday night. Authorities at Kootenai Medical Center say the man had no identification on him and has not been reported missing locally. If anyone has any information leading to John Doe's identity, please contact Kootenai County authorities. Charges are not being filed against the pizza delivery driver, who suffered a broken arm."

That was all it took, one radio blurb to introduce me to John Doe. Who was he? Where was his family? Why had they not discovered his absence yet?

I parked my car in a small gravel lot behind Whitaker Jewelry, the store my family has owned and operated for three generations. I bypassed the shop, eyeing a display piece in the window case that needed better placement, making a mental note to rearrange it first thing; however, not before my morning ritual of orange juice and a scone at Dickson's Coffee next door.

"Good morning, Henry," I smiled maturely.

Henry, the owner and barista, handed me a bottled juice and scone without question. "Banana-nut wheat germ."

I held my gut.

"Fiber," he patted his chest. Henry survived a very public heart attack last year, in this very spot, and has since eliminated the doughnuts from the menu.

I handed him four dollars. He leaned forward and whispered, "Your dad let me in on the secret. If you need anything at all, I'm a wall away." It was comforting to know that although I was totally alone, someone was aware of me, unlike poor John Doe.

"Six-week cruise? Up the canal?" Henry whistled, as if impressed.

"Spain to Amsterdam. Don't think about it. It's sickening, really--wine, Europe, the canals--it's just wrong." I grabbed my drink and significantly heavy pastry bag and turned toward the door. "My heart thanks you."

"Among other things," Henry winked.

With my hands full, I keyed into Whitaker Jewelry. I flipped on the lights and nearly tripped over the newspaper that had been dropped through the front door mail slot. Rolled up and wrapped in plastic, I tossed the *North Idaho Press* on top of the glass counter, with my juice and scone, and immediately keyed into the window display case. The placement was backwards, with the newest engagement setting in the back corner and cuff links stealing center stage. I rearranged the jewelry and heard the front-door bell jingle.

Julie walked in, her tall figure somewhat drooping as she just hovered near the door.

"I already said goodbye," I said, trying to stave off a smile.

"I came back for another load of essentials for the dorm, and when I drove down Sherman, my car automatically pulled over. I had no control, I swear," she said.

Julie spotted the ring in my hand. "Is this the newest one?" She slid it on her finger, twisting it in the light. Julie was the only person outside my family who knew that I design jewelry under the pen name *Lenora*, a secret my dad insisted on when I was twelve. "What's his name?"

"No name," I admitted. All my pieces have a name, known only to me, my family and Julie. "I was thinking of 'Leaf,' short for 'Leaving.'"

"I'm not the one who betrayed our agreement," Julie pointed out.

We were fifteen when we made the college pact. "A lot changes in three years," I reminded her.

"Well, running sucks without you."

"I hate pain," I said.

"You know you'll miss it, the pain and all." Julie put her arms around me and hugged me one last time. "I'm only an hour and a half away."

"I know. I was there two weeks ago moving you in."

"I expect you at the finish line of my first race," she said. I nodded and took the ring back from her.

"I've got to go before I get all weird again." Julie turned out the door. I saw her Volkswagen bug loaded with clothes, shoes, her favorite stuffed teddy bear, and a large colorful floor lamp roped to the top of the roof. She sped off, honking.

It was supposed to be the best six weeks of my life, with Mom and Dad gone and at eighteen, all the freedom in the world. I had known for months of their trans-European cruise, as Dad had prepped me with every detail on running the shop without him. Dad has been the owner and Mom and I have been the sole employees my entire life. Dad had been meaning to retire at sixty-five, two years ago, and yet had no one to offer the family business to, no one who desired to take it on, besides my under-aged self.

Now that I am finally of age, Dad has considered the possibility of retirement. Their cruise was a test run for me. I am the exact opposite of my half-sister Dawn. Dawn is the byproduct of my father's childhood marriage that lasted two years. Dad was young, just nineteen, when he married his first wife who ran away two years after their marriage, leaving eighteen-month-old Dawn with him. Single and still a kid himself, he raised her the best he could. Dawn's one and only child from marriage number two, Donny, is the closest thing I have to a sibling, although I wouldn't call us close.

For some, life presents second chances. At forty-eight, Dad met Mom at his thirtieth high-school reunion and found the soul mate he never had. They married within six weeks. To the total shock and dismay of everyone, I was born nine months later. They say I was the miracle child and another second chance for Dad. He promised to raise his second daughter right, and discovered the key was spending as much time with me as possible. Working at the shop made it easy to get the time in. Since I can remember, I've watched Dad pour hot silver and gold into premade wax molds that he ordered from a catalogue. I inquisitively studied the discarded wax that he threw out after every piece. Dad tolerated my piddling around the back studio, and at eleven I reshaped the wax into a Father's Day tie pin that Dad had thought would turn out to be a childhood art experiment, but revealed to him a true talent in me. He displayed the pin in the window case titled *Father's Fusion* and sold forty-three that week to locals. From then on, Dad allowed me to create special holiday pieces and designs of the month, a hobby that came very naturally to me.

I realized that my tinkering was more than a hobby when I received my first request for a one-of-a-kind engagement ring. A semi-pro golfer who was staying at the Coeur d'Alene Resort and enjoying the unique Coeur d'Alene greens came by the shop and requested a ring to be made in the shape of a golf tee with a golf ball diamond on top, apparently for his European-model girlfriend. Money was no object. His one request was that no other ring be made like it. I quickly sketched the design on paper, and once my sketch and his ideas found common ground, he made a fifty percent deposit, and added a thousand-dollar tip for allowing him to keep the original mold. The ring was astonishing, and his girlfriend wore the ring in her latest magazine spread. The ring was noticed, and Whitaker Jewelry gained national attention. Queries came in furiously about the designer. Mom and Dad insisted that a plain childhood was better than celebrity, and if I wanted any chance at normalcy, I must create a private designer name, a nom de plum of sorts. I chose Lenora for no other reason than I liked the way the name rolled off my tongue, and I loved making cursive Ls. *Designs by Lenora* single-handedly saved the shop, Dad once said. Lenora received several personal inquiries, which I enjoyed responding to. The outdated store became a couture tourist stop, and I was a simple counter girl by day, designer by night. I didn't mind the obscurity, really. I like keeping secrets.

With the income I made, Dad insisted on putting most of it into a savings account for college, and yet I told him the money needed to go to the shop's upkeep. The carpet was old, the glass displays were original, and the security was lacking. After a break-in a year ago, Dad finally agreed to having the place updated and secured, hiring my cousin Donny and his friends to do the wiring.

I can talk to Dad about everything, and talk him *into* anything. That is why I convinced him to let me turn the upstairs storage of Whitaker Jewelry into my own studio loft. It was abandoned as an apartment sixty years ago, but with my vision and persistence, it was easily renovated into my personal abode. I'm not sure what I liked better, the cozy cramped quarters above the store, or the idea that I was replicating a really old novel. Sometimes I read by candlelight, providing ethereal ambiance that I imagined the Bronte sisters wrote their masterpieces amidst. I loved my drab little loft and didn't have any regret about not going to college. I'm perfectly content with all I have, and even accepting of what I lack.

A jewelry store is one of the most romantic places to work, but the least likely place to meet anyone available, for obvious reasons. The men in my life are, well, truthfully, those I read about. And if they are really impressive, I'll name a ring after them. My father always told me that if a guy's worth anything, he will do whatever it takes to win you. Maybe his thinking was a bit old-fashioned, but I knew that it would happen this way for me. No singles' groups or chat rooms. I would hold out if I had to, until I was forty-eight, like my mother, to let the right one find me.

In the meantime, I put all my energy into Whitaker Jewelry, managing the store and moonlighting as Lenora. I was thrilled that Dad had finally set a date to hand over the reigns, and the title to the business, on his sixty-eighth birthday next year. Mom deserved to live her golden years with him, enjoying all the things that small business owners never get the chance to do, like travel. I should mention that all of my talent didn't just appear out of nowhere; my mom is a talented painter. She can capture warmth through her acrylics that nearly radiate heat. I've grown up with her vivid canvases on every wall of our home. That is the only place her work is displayed. After marrying Dad, she never pursued her art as anything but a hobby.

And that is why I suspect that my refusal to go to college was such a sore subject between Mom and myself. Both my parents had not attended, and Mom felt like her opportunities in art were stifled by a lack of marketing skills which college could have provided. She feels that there is never such a thing as a wasted education. I finally convinced Mom that managing a family-run business didn't require four years of an education at some institution, but an apprenticeship in person. So, as this summer neared an end and it was clear I wasn't going to budge, Mom started to accept that I wasn't college-bound. I transitioned into my new life by working with Dad full time.

After bidding them bon voyage, and sending off Julie again, I was finally alone. Alone to be me, free from any assignments, homework, monotonous tasks that had no point but to claim mastery of grammar, mathematics, or scientific theory. I was free to be one hundred percent me. I soaked up the last sunny days of August in the shop devouring novels when foot traffic was slow, and creating a new Lenora one-of-a-kind at night. I cooked for myself using exotic oils and spices, and enjoyed the freedom of space and time. And, I developed a daily fascination with John Doe. The hospital PR department released daily solicitations for information regarding his identity to the news, in the paper, and on the radio. This stranger invaded my every thought, stole my attention and quickly became a private obsession. Day after day, I would key into the shop, set down my juice and scone, and immediately tear open the newspaper. *Had he awakened? Did his family find him? Any employers report him missing? How could anybody be so unnoticed in this world?* I would say little prayers in my heart for him, prayers that he would heal and be found. After about ten minutes of drifting, I would force myself to shut the paper and move on.

****

Nothing was too different about this particular Monday morning, except for two things: Mom and Dad had been gone for a week now, and it was my nineteenth birthday. Nineteen is an insignificant year, I decided. Not quite considered adult by society's standards, and nothing really special to claim. People start a career or a degree. It's an in-between age. I didn't feel any different, except for that private, magical feeling I held every year on my birthday. Although I had started to feel very grown up by moving out of my parents' home and into the loft this summer, today was going to be the true test of adult maturity, being alone. Most adults I know avoid acknowledging their birthdays, so I would do the same. No birthday breakfast this year with Mom. Just a four-mile morning jog around Tubbs Hill, as I do every morning.

Tubbs Hill is an endearing local landmark in Coeur d'Alene. Jetting out into the water, this 120-acre forested, public-owned property sits next to the Coeur d'Alene Resort, with dirt trails winding away from all civilization in a two-mile loop showcasing the lake, the mountains, the beautiful white pines and the native shrubbery. It's also a killer trail run. I run the loop two times every morning, rain or shine.

This particular morning, the lake was glass reflecting red and green foliage, the perfect birthday gift in itself. I hate racing; however, I love running. I love the crisp air in my lungs, the tension in my toes pushing up each rocky incline. I love the mud streaks that paint themselves on my calves. I love the physical strain on my body. Above all, I love the escape--the feverish thoughts and feelings, the conversations in my head, the dreaming. The morning run was the first of many rituals that I had christened my new adult life with.

After my run and shower, I routinely exit the loft down the back stairs, which dumps into a two-car gravel parking lot and the block's dumpster. I could come down the loft stairs and make a quick right to open the attached rear door to Whitaker Jewelry, but entering the front of the store felt like entering work, not just an extension of my apartment. To me, they were two different buildings.

Continuing with my morning ritual, I made my way to Dickson's Coffee, ordering my daily OJ, along with a molasses-pumpkin scone. I keyed myself into the shop, disarming the store. Like an obsessed fan, I grabbed the morning paper, ripped off the plastic, shuffled to the back of the local section, and scanned for his story. *More wolf tags offered... Public urged to attend levy vote today... Local Ironman prepares for Kona...* I flipped the page and kept scanning, until I found it squeezed between ads for financial counseling: *John Doe needs your help.*

The front bell jingled, and a young couple sheepishly strolled in. *Monday morning engagement traffic,* I thought to myself. The young couple couldn't hide it if they tried. I hid my breakfast and newspaper behind the counter.

I could read a person like a fortuneteller reads the thickness of your wallet, and the young couple hesitantly entering the store was an easy read. "I'm guessing a '*Congratulations*' is in order."

He was a tall kid, probably my age, and much too young to be engaged, I thought. "I had planned to come see you *before* I proposed. I'm sure you've heard that one before," he smiled bashfully.

"Sometimes," I answered. "But now she can get what she wants, right?" I was already sizing up the couple, making judgments that would help with the sale. They were an impulsive pair, I assessed.

"You're Maggie, right?" he said out of the blue. "Trig, Mr. Hammond. You were a junior, my senior year." I couldn't place him, and it was a bit awkward. "Chris Steenberg," he said. "I sat in the back corner by the window."

"Oh, right. I thought you looked familiar." To be fair, my junior year was a blur. I spent every waking moment either on the track or in the shop, designing as Lenora.

"This is Elena. We met at the University of Montana." Elena was petite with sharp-sculpted eyebrows.

Elena offered her hand, "Nice to meet you." I accepted the cordiality, shaking her pencil-thin fingers, while I studied her for just a moment. I had nearly mastered the art of picking out the perfect engagement setting on the first try, another talent, my dad had insisted. If I could take ten seconds to get in the head of the bride-to-be, I could find a match.

I glanced from Elena to the case, walking slowly down the displays looking, searching for her first pick. "So, you just got engaged last night?" I asked, while searching for her match.

"It was perfect," the polished brunette said. "He did so great."

If anything in the world seems insincere, it was a woman who critiqued her own proposal, as if she were judging a figure-skating performance. She needed the story. The WOW factor mattered to her. I knew this type of woman and gave them five years at tops. I also knew that this woman needed a show ring, not a practical ring, not to even mention the poor guy's budget, but a ring that forced the world to notice her.

"Asscher cut, platinum, high setting," I mumbled to myself. "Rhett, you're the one." I pulled a shimmering, square-cut setting out from the glass and held the box for approval.

"Oh, my," Elena gushed. "Can I?"

I slid the ring out of the box and handed it to Chris. "Go for it."

The young man took a breath, and gently slid the ring on Elena's finger. The diamond immediately fell over on her tiny finger. She held the ring in place, with the huge diamond on top. "I'm going to cry," she said. Like clockwork, she held her hand out, examined it in all directions to catch the sunlight, and knew that she could never part from it. There were tears in her eyes, no kidding.

"We'll size it for you," I assured her.

"Its perfect, exactly what I would have chosen. I don't need to try on anything else." I watched as Chris Steenberg clinched his jaw, maybe in anxiety, maybe in the dizzying material decisions facing him, a foretaste of the years to come.

I sized her finger, writing down size 5 ¼ on an invoice.

"I'm glad you like it." I admired their love, even if I knew it was doomed. Rhett was doomed too, the moment he met Scarlet in *Gone with the Wind*. He would fight for her feverishly, until he had the strength to walk away.

"Will I be able to afford a honeymoon?" Chris said, hinting sincerity.

I had learned long ago never to talk about money directly. "If you wouldn't mind stepping back here, I'll just have you fill out the paperwork." He followed me to the register while Elena scoured the glass case, often examining the dazzling ring on her left finger.

I spoke in a low tone to Chris, almost in a whisper. "This is a Lenora original, making the setting two thousand, but the flawless stone is where the real damage comes in. We can reset the setting with an imperfect stone. We do it all the time." I had a way of helping men save face, which somehow made me an even more natural saleswoman.

"Imperfect stone?" he questioned.

"This stone is flawless grade, which basically means they have no blemishes under ten time's magnification. We can reset it with a SI1, which is an imperfect stone, but unless she's a diamond grader, she'll never notice. Same size, same cut. That will shave off two thousand. If you want any lesser grade, you'll have to go to the mall."

Looking at his fiancé admiring her hand, "I don't think she cares about the grade, just as long as it's big. You have payment plans?"

"Of course, I can have it resized and reset by Friday. At that time I will need a deposit of $1,000."

"Forgive me for asking, but the diamonds are from . . ." Chris looked at his feet. "I don't want to make an impulsive choice. I've heard stories, and it would be nice knowing the origin," Chris said.

I looked at Chris Steenberg, astonished at his question. Most people don't care where their diamonds come from or how they get them.

"All of our diamonds are laser registered from our supplier in Canada. Your purchase is a clean one," I assured him. Dad had decided to deal only with Canada, to subdue his hurting conscience, after discovering his past business had included several blood diamonds. *It's never too late to make good changes*, he would tell me.

"The laser registration number will be on your final receipt, and we'll keep one here on file too. Don't hesitate to come in and get the setting checked for looseness, or the stone cleaned, or when you're ready to add an anniversary band," I mentioned, while handing him a receipt.

He looked completely overwhelmed. Elena looked completely in love. I held the box out and she contrived sadness when returning the ring. "I'll call when it's ready. Again, congratulations."

I wondered how this woman snagged this guy. *He was really thoughtful. Why didn't I notice him in high school?* I often talk in my head. *Remember, he chose her. What does that say about him?* I had a tendency to judge love, to size up couples and wonder what their attraction stemmed from. In cases like this, it seemed so mismatched, to see a man love a woman, and then notice that she's in love with the attention that accompanies love. She has a Rhett, and she doesn't even know it.

The moment the couple left, I dove for the paper that I had tossed under the counter, and ripped through page after page, scanning. There it was, second page of the local section, next to a colored ad of fried bacon and eggs atop a scramble of potatoes:

John Doe Needs Your Help

The man Kootenai Medical Center is calling John Doe who was struck by a car nine days ago in downtown Wallace is still in a medically-induced coma at KMC while doctors monitor swelling of the brain. The man, presumed to be in his twenties, had no identification on him, and witnesses say he jetted out into oncoming traffic without warning. Medical personnel have

handed jurisdiction over to
Kootenai County authorities in
hopes that local or even national
missing person's reports will fit
John Doe's description. So far, no
claims have been filed. If you
have any information leading to
John Doe's identity, please call
local authorities.

I spent the next hour glaring into the magnification glass removing the Rhett stone with pliers, thinking about this man. Who was he? Where were his parents, his family, or even his friends? The saddest, most tragic thought was hard for me to imagine: How could someone fight for their life all alone?

The phone rang, breaking my silent quandary. "Happy birthday, Darling!" It was the familiar voice of my mother, static and far away.

"Mom!"

My mother raved about their nautical adventures, which landed them currently in Northern Spain. "I missed our breakfast, Mags. Dad and I are having a toast in your honor right now. Cariñena. a beautiful, red Spanish wine." She sounded a bit too happy. "Don't tell me you are spending your birthday in the shop?"

"It *is* Monday, Mom. I'm here every Monday."

"A shut-in on your birthday. I feel guilty that we didn't bring you with us."

"First, I would not want to be part of your anniversary cruise. Eww! And second, don't knock the loft." I am much more like Dad in this respect. I love small places and my daily predictable routine.

"Oh for goodness sakes, Mags, I'm going to have your father fire you when we get back if you don't get out a little more. I worry about you, all alone."

"What are you talking about? I'm surrounded by lots of beautiful men," I slid Elena's ring on my finger, admiring it. "Besides, I'm too good for you to fire. I just sold Rhett."

"The Asscher?"

"Yep. With an SI1 though."

"Darling, I've got to go. Dad sends his love. Why don't you call Donny?"

"Bye, Mom." I kissed her through the phone, and hung up. The thought of spending my birthday with Donny was depressing. Dawn's son Donny is technically my nephew, but being five months my senior, for all intents and purposes, we established ourselves as cousins early on. You wouldn't know he is older. I have spent my fair share parenting him these past four years: picking him up from overnight parties before Dad had to, restocking his school lunch credit since his lunch allowance never made it into the right hands, and single-handedly accomplishing graduation for him by reworking his senior project at the eleventh hour so that he could earn a D+. Dawn acts more like a buddy than a mother, and he hasn't overcome his innate love for all things loud, dangerous, and illegal. If you don't find him working at the Ski & Skate Shop, or hunting, motocrossing, or snowboarding, you could put sure money that he's lounging in his 800-square-foot rental life-lined to his video game of the year. Never alone, he has an entourage of gaming addicts who have wired his place for every upgrade, surround sound, subwoofers, digital this or that. You can get dizzy just stepping in his house, and you certainly risk hearing loss. I don't get the draw, but apparently it acts as a siren to every techno male who hears the call.

Donny and his computer-genius pal Victor put their technical skills to some use by wiring the jewelry store with alarms and cameras during the shop's remodel. Dad thought maybe Donny was ready to step-it-up, be a man, and embrace responsible living. Dad even offered to give Donny a job, but told him he expected him to arrive to work clean and sober every morning. Donny declined the offer.

I have nearly reached the end of my compassion for Donny, so spending the beginning of my true adult life with someone who lives off the backs of others did not appeal to me.

I set the Rhett down, sans its diamond, to resize it later today. I deposited the flawless diamond into a velvet receptacle and secured it in our safe in the back. I knew I wasn't focused enough to do my best work, since John Doe was still knocking on my brain. I attempted to distract myself by spot-checking each jewelry piece under the glass. *Louie L'Amour* is rough, jagged, and rustic. *Jay Gatsby* is jazz-age, sweeping curves, flaunting yet tragic. *Gilbert Blythe* is country sweet and harmless. *Rhett Butler* is impressive, antique, Southern charm. Out of all my designs, I like *Atticus Finch* the most, an understated band of diamonds which shouts simplicity and strength. Each setting unique, these are my romantic leads, the men in my life that each represent qualities I consider a must: chivalry, faithfulness, courage, tenderness, optimism.

It was with these men that I had planned to spend my nineteenth birthday. I had no idea what was really in store.

Chapter Two: Tsunami

I dreamed my way through the day, resetting and sizing the engagement ring, Rhett. My stomach reminded me that it was closing time, demanding attention. I never did finish reading the morning paper, so I shoved the *North Idaho Press* into my purse to finish at home. I exited from the front, as usual, locking up behind me after setting the alarm.

Couples strolled down Sherman Avenue, hand in hand. A group of junior high girls in beach-wear and flip flops huddled together, giggling and scanning for familiar faces. There seemed to be at least an hour of sunlight left, and I hesitated to shut myself in the loft for the night. Having the secret of my birthday locked up in the loft lacked adventure. I'd surprise my mom and take her advice. I'd go out to dinner on my birthday. At that, I walked down Sherman Avenue and crossed the street.

Chinese Gardens, nestled across the street from the sleepy Song Bird Theatre and adjacent to a tattoo parlor, has been my favorite hole-in-the-wall restaurant since I can remember. I sat in the red vinyl booth alongside the window and ordered egg drop soup, along with chow mein and my favorite, sweet-and-sour chicken.

Condensation settled on the corners of the window, and I sat watching the passers-by. Across the street, on an old water-stained park bench, an attractive young couple sat down, the kind that look good together--the kind that look like a pair. The girl was crying. I made up the back story in my head: *They'd just had a fight over something catastrophic, like another woman, and they were at the peak of their decision to stick together or walk away forever.* Gently, the young man put his arm around her and began to stroke her back. He said nothing. She sobbed, and he sat somber, placing the other hand on her knee. *No, this wasn't about another woman. This was fear. She was sick, or he was sick. Words covered guilt. The silence between the two of them determined a more tender, unanswerable sadness. Maybe she lost a parent, or a child--maybe their first unborn child?*

Whatever grief they were facing, I oddly envied them. He communicated everything through the stroke of his hand. How lucky she was to have him, another soul, to be a support in her need. I stirred my soup aimlessly as the chow mein and chicken arrived, and with the warm smile of my waitress telling me to "Enjoy," I felt more alone than ever before. My throat began to swell. A dry hotness ran down my neck. *Don't cry. This is stupid.*

A tension in my innermost soul emerged, to defy this haunting loneliness on my birthday. I looked out the window and saw the couple had left. With a quick scan, I spotted them down one block, arm in arm, walking. I stared in numbness, feeling abandoned at the scene. The room buzzed as couples, families, even single diners seemed to enjoy their meals. I watched the double doors of the kitchen swing open, and the chef was dropping crab rangoon into hot oil. The waitress was bustling through the kitchen with teacups and a large pot of green tea balanced on an overloaded tray, somehow managing a safe delivery. I finished my soup and boxed the rest. I wasn't that hungry after all. As I reached in my purse to pull out my wallet, the morning paper spilled out onto the floor. I picked it up, my eye catching on that familiar headline: "John Doe Needs Your Help."

Looking back, it's irrational what made me decide to visit him that night, rather inexcusable for *how* I managed to visit him. But for a nineteen-year-old girl, it wasn't irrational at all. All I knew was that something in me was pulling me to him, calling me to help. And it felt right. I can't make all wrongs in this world right, but I could make a difference. John Doe would not die alone.

I walked into the entrance of the hospital with only one thing on my mind, to comfort John Doe. I wasn't sure how the process of seeing a visitor worked. The last time I had been here was nineteen years to the day. I was a lucky kid, with two insanely protective parents. I approached the visitor's counter and was greeted by a triage receptionist. "What can I do for you?"

"I'm here to see John Doe."

She stared at me a moment. Her eyes widened, as if she just registered what I said. "Oh. Great. I just need you to register. Family will have special extended visiting hours, of course. I'll let his doctors know you're here." She pushed paperwork over the counter and picked up the phone.

"I'm not family," I interrupt.

A look of disappointment shattered her enthusiasm, as she hung up the phone. "The

NEURO/ICU is only for family. Are you a reporter?" The accusation stirred a defensive need in me to not be turned away. "Our PR department sends a press update every night."

Without warning, an earthquake of a lie erupted from within, the words spewing like hot lava. "Yet! I'm not family, yet. I'm his fiancé."

They say you can't stop a wave once it's started. The tsunami was on its way. "Fiancé?" The receptionist hesitated, returning to her apologetic smile. "Let me call the doctor." The double doors buzzed open.

I was immediately met by a nurse who looked more like a surgeon, covered in blue masks and scrubs, who led me to the Intensive Care Unit. I trailed behind, realizing I had just crossed a line that was not mine to cross.

****

Mira was a mid-thirty neuro nurse who hated her job, and it showed. Being around so much sadness just sort of rubs off on you, she shared with me once. Mira showed me to John Doe's room. She took his chart off the door, pausing before entering. "You've been briefed of his condition?"

"No." I could hardly speak.

Mira looked tired, but empathetic. "I'll get Dr. James to brief you on his prognosis."

"Can I just sit with him for now?" I definitely didn't want to know too much.

"All right, just know he's roughed up a bit--a lot." She led me to his bedside.

I quietly tiptoed behind her and immediately looked for his face. All I could see was his black eyelashes. He was completely wrapped in gauze, mummified. At the base of his neck was the yellow staining of iodine. His body lay still, leaving only the melodic symphony of machines breathing for him, ventilating oxygen into his lungs through a tube inserted in his throat. I saw bloodied scabs on his neck, in his ears, and on his hand, which was resting on the sheet. I felt nauseated; a wave of heat stemming from my stomach flowed up to my neck and down my legs.

"I'll leave you for a minute," Mira whispered. She left the room, but I could feel her stare on my back for longer than a moment.

I stood close to John Doe, not daring to touch him in his fragile state. My heart was racing, as I was face to face with the man I had been reading about, thinking about, praying for. Feeling like a voyeur in my silence, I felt it oddly appropriate to introduce myself. "Hi. I'm Maggie. Margaret. Margaret Claire. I don't generally do this sort of thing." I felt silly, trying to rationalize my visit. He was feeble and fragile, the machines doing all the work for him. "I hope you're not too scared. They tell me you're in good hands." I stopped, realizing the futility of having a one-sided conversation with a man whom I'm not acquainted with. Yet, somehow the bandages created a barrier, a way for me to continue talking to the mummified man. "I want to tell you a secret: Today's my birthday. I'm all alone. Sort of makes us a pair, huh?"

The last comment sat with me a little heavy. I was being absurd. My loneliness was self-induced, unlike his. I needed to leave. Get up and leave right now. Don't wait until the doctor comes. Leave now. They can call me later if they need to, and I can tell them that it was the wrong guy. I stood up and walked toward the door, and just before leaving, added, "Good luck to you, John Doe. I'm rooting for you." As I turned toward the door I heard a faint cough, almost a choke.

A pace away from the door, I turned to look at him. His chest jolted. *The tsunami is approaching land. Get to high ground, now.* His chest raised high, slowly deflated. *A riptide. I'm being pulled in.* I floated back to him, put my hand on his chest, and gently began rubbing his shoulder. Words evaded me. My hand followed his shoulder down his arm, until my hand landed in his. I held his hand. Could he be squeezing it? Or maybe the tension in my body was moving to my fingers.

"I don't mean to interrupt," whispered a low, fatherly voice from behind. "I'm Dr. James." He was wearing a lanyard with the clearance badge identifying Carl James, KMC neurosurgeon. "I'm picking up some activities on the monitor that I want to check. It would be best if you stepped outside for just a moment." Dr. James got busy to work, testing breathing tubes and charting numbers.

I backed out, to find Mira approaching with a rolling registration computer.

"I've got just a few questions that I need to get started, and then another nurse may take over. I'm off in ten minutes," she said. "First of all, and most curious to us all, is his name."

The peaceful water that the riptide had dragged me to way out in the ocean went from silent to a rumbling roar. The tsunami was here. I was dizzy, weak, and confused by my desire to ride the wave. The force picked me up and smashed me onto the sand, relentless. *What is his name? John Doe.* I had called him this in the week of conversing with him in my mind. *John Doe. J.D., J.D., J.D.* Off the cuff, I forged, "J-ackson D-arren."

"Jackson Darren." Mira typed it in.

"Jack," I offered.

"Birthdate?"

Quick math . . . mid-twenties . . . "February 7, nineteen eighty . . . six."

"Address and phone?"

"He lives with me. We live together." Now I was out of my mind. I have no idea what had overtaken me, except the adrenaline rush of playing the game. *Just tell the truth and run. Run now,* the rational side of my conscience told me, but an even stronger instinct wouldn't allow it. John Doe has a family, someone to hold his hand in silence for the first time. I gave Mira the address and phone to Whitaker Jewelry.

"Contact information for his parents or living relatives?"

"They are all back East."

"We still need to know living relatives, since you technically aren't family yet."

"Deceased." I was grabbing at straws. "His parents are deceased. He's got some relatives back East, but I've never met them. I don't even have contact info."

"Any siblings?"

"No." *The nurse is looking at me; she's figuring out I'm a scam.*

"Off the record, can I ask you one question?" Mira took her hands off the keyboard and twiddled her fingers.

Guilty, but let me explain, I wanted to confess, but the tsunami was back for a second strike.

"Why did it take you so long to get here? He--Jack--has *needed you,* and it's been a week.

Where were you?" Mira looked me in the eyes, and I could see her heartbreak, the same heartbreak I had felt when reading John Doe's story. I concluded then, at this moment, that I represented hope, and family, not only to John Doe but to all the staff who have carried the burden of being his surrogate family. My presence was an obvious release to many who have worked around the clock to extend his life.

The room was spinning. I was in too deep. Why do all tragic characters come to an end? I envisioned Scarlet and Rhett yelling at each other; Jay Gatsby and Daisy confessing their affair to her husband; Jane Eyre running away from Mr. Rochester; Sophie and Nathan in their final demise, and I suddenly burst out, "We had a fight, and I told him to leave." I couldn't believe I was playing the part. Even more, I was *feeling* the part, trembling, drowning in dizzying lies, and believing them.

Mira uncharacteristically embraced me. And that is all I remember, except that Mira's arms cut into my underarms, twisting my shoulder while helping to break the fall.

Seconds or minutes passed, I'm not sure exactly. I could hear hushed voices talking over me. "I was just asking her questions and she appeared extremely overwhelmed . . . MIA because of a domestic altercation," Mira was briefing those standing nearby.

"No more questions for now." Dr. James was still here, as I saw him when I first opened my eyes. He was very handsome; gray peppered his dark hair, adding to his natural warmth. "Maggie," he put his hand on my shoulder, offering compassion, "this is a very emotional and traumatic experience for family, for loved ones. I am going to do my best to make sure that Jack is safe. We want you to make sure that you are okay. The nurses have some support services for you that you should consider. We're all in this together."

I sensed a longing on Mira's face as she looked at the doctor, a look I couldn't quite place, but one of sadness and adoration all at the same time. Mira had pain under her tough exterior, and with that demeanor she kneeled toward me and whispered to Dr. James, "I've got it from here." Dr. James exchanged a controlled glance at Mira, then stood up and walked away. A shift in the nurse's mood toward me, a new loyalty to me, bonded us in that moment. She offered to walk me to my car. I didn't need protecting. I knew what I needed; I needed to get out of here, get to dry land.

Mira wouldn't take no for an answer. I told her I could find my car just fine, but she walked me to the parking lot anyway. As I fumbled for my keys, I cordially thanked her for her concern. She wasn't going to allow me to escape so easily.

"Look, I've been working in the neuro unit for nine years now, and I know the reality of these cases. It's tough on everybody, not just the patient. You do have someone to go home to, someone who can stay with you tonight?"

"Yes," I lied.

Mira handed me a folder filled with brochures on grieving, trauma, and even one on loss and recovery. I accepted them, although I knew I would never read them.

"Mira, can I ask you one thing?"

"Anything."

"Is he going to die? What I mean is, were you--the hospital--Dr. James--just keeping him alive so that he could die after family arrived--after I arrived?"

Mira took a moment before answering, as if planning her words carefully. "It is really comforting, to all of us, to see you here. The reality is his injuries are very serious. We do the best we can to support life. And we'll keep doing the best we can."

She was dodging my question, which in turn answered it. Of course they were happy to see me. Now they could take the burden of responsibility off of themselves and allow me to carry it, allow me to make those life-or-death decisions.

I got in the car, knowing the only thing I could do was escape. I needed to clear my head, find the solace of a warm bath, a comforting book, and the privacy of my loft. I could muster the courage to figure this out once I got to my safe abode.

It was a short drive from the hospital to Sherman Avenue, but raining nonetheless. A warm summer storm was always a highlight for me, but I couldn't celebrate it tonight. As regretful as I was for deceiving the hospital staff and bringing false hope to an entire hospital community, there was something in me that didn't want to let him go. I felt a spark inside, a connection to this stranger. My short little visit provided a reason to leave my fantasy world of heroes and heroines behind and start living for John Doe, or Jack, as I would now call him. I would rather believe that his exhale, his short burst of energy, was his way of bidding me to stay, instead of just showing *some activity on the monitor,* as the doctor phrased it.

I keyed myself in the back door and made it up the fifteen wooden steps to my loft. I threw on the lights and jumped back five paces, hitting my head on the wall as four grown men jumped out at me.

Chapter Three: Nineteen

"Surprise!" shouted the four intruders. My heart stopped momentarily until shooting streams of adrenaline jumpstarted it again. I immediately identified my cousin Donny.

"Donny!" I rubbed my head where I knocked into the wall.

"Happy Birthday, M.C."

Still holding my head, I mumbled, "Mom call you?"

"Have a little faith in me, Cuz'," Donny bragged.

His best friend Wyn spilled the beans, "She wired him one hundred bucks." Wyn smirked at me, before adding, "How's it going, Whitaker?"

I was surprised to see Wyn in town. Last I heard he was in Fairbanks, Alaska, playing amateur ball for the Goldpanners.

"You gave in for a hundred bucks? Donny, your time is worth more than that," I scoffed.

Donny glared at Wyn. "I got you a cake, Mags. Everyone needs a cake on their birthday. That's what you've always preached."

"Homemade or store-bought?" I quizzed, to see if Donny really did take note.

He looked at Wyn, busted again. "What kind of cake did I *make* her, Wyn?"

"You *made* her lemon chiffon, Donny. Remember squeezing the fresh lemon juice and zesting the peel?"

"Zest isn't a verb. You grate the peel to remove the zest. Please tell me you bought the cake. Who knows what could be in there if it was made at your house."

"Our house," Wyn corrected. "I moved in last week."

"I thought you were up North." Wyn was sporting blue Dickies and his very own name badge on a grease-monkey shirt.

"I found a job here. It works." His grimy hands told the story.

"Quick Lube," Donny cracked himself up. "I just want to say it all day. The goddamn Quick Lube." The two other unfamiliar men looked bored out of their minds until now, one redhead and the other dishwater blond.

"Do they have any openings?" the redhead asked, then busted his gut, along with the others.

Ignoring his crudeness, Wyn answered, "You have to be able to pass a test."

I didn't exactly like how these strangers made themselves at home on my couch. "Did Donny pay you guys too?"

"Name's Red."

"Fitting. I will tell Mom and Dad that we had a wonderful visit, and thanks for the party. You guys can go. I've got a lot on my mind." I gave Donny a glance that made it clear he was to leave.

The blond finally spoke. "Tequila, anyone?" He held up a bottle of some cheap, amber liquid.

"Nope," I cut him off.

From the kitchen came a very familiar voice that made my heart jump. "No one is leaving before a toast!" It was Julie, holding up a shot glass. Behind her trailed yet another stranger, a tall, leggy man with a handsome olive complexion.

"Julie!" I stood frozen, as the one person I truly wanted to see was now here, in my loft.

"You know I wouldn't miss your birthday!" she said. Julie had the personality of a fuzzy kitten and an energetic kangaroo. As hyper as she appeared, she had proven to be the most loyal and trustworthy confidante anyone could ask for in a friend. "Corbin, I want you to meet Maggie, my friend, the reclusive artist," and aside to him she added, "who *should* be running with us." She then introduced, "Maggie, this is Corbin. He's a teammate and, well, my ride." I noted the sparkle in her eye.

"It's nice to finally meet you, Maggie. You run the jewelry store?" Corbin asked formally.

"You're standing on it."

Donny was helping himself to my music collection and pulled out the one and only artist that we share a common interest in: Janis Joplin. He turned the bass up and filled my loft with her throaty tunes.

Amidst all the chaos of the last ten minutes, I was nearly able to subdue the confusion in my head concerning John Doe. If anyone could help make sense of my infraction, Julie could. All I needed was to get the four unwelcomed guests out of my loft.

Donny finished pouring the shots and passed around glasses, "A toast to the birthday girl." Suddenly, an innocent drink didn't seem to be the worst thing I had done tonight, and if it was the precipitator to making this party move on and move out, I was more than willing.

Julie began, "To a remarkable friend, Margaret Claire, on your nineteenth birthday. Nineteen. . ." She paused to think of something witty to say about nineteen. "Okay, nineteen is kind of lame." Julie continued with artificial regality, "May remarkable things encounter you; may you find peace, love and joy this year; and for all the good men in this world's sake, may you put down your books, lock up the store, venture away from Whitaker Jewelry and have one last teen-aged adventure."

"Adventure!" Donny said, as his unknown guests added a "Booyah!" Wyn discreetly set aside his drink.

"Cheers," I was last to join, and sipped the shot down slowly, trying to hide the dry cough in the back of my throat.

The blond poured another shot into my glass the moment it parted from my lips. "Who are you?" Then, to Donny aloud, "Who is he?" I was trying my best to be cordial, regardless if doing shots was completely opposite my common practice.

"You know Victor. We wired this place during the remodel."

"Right. I really shouldn't be--Cheers." I pulled back my head to allow the tequila to slide down my throat as quickly as possible, hoping that maybe this time a faster gulp would diffuse the urge to spew it all back out. The rush instantly hit me, so I figured I had better say this quickly: "Even though you broke into my loft and invaded my space, Donny, Wyn, and you two," I couldn't remember the strangers' names, "thanks for showing up. Julie, Corbin, thank you."

"You're welcome." Julie obviously hadn't wasted time in college learning the ropes. She was encouraging a third round.

I watched in disbelief. "Is this what you've learned in college?" I asked. Victor was pouring another in my glass as I contemplated the glowing liquid. "I can't"--and I dumped the drink back down my throat, --"drink another sip! I'm done." That one went to my head, quickly. My vision was fogging, and disorientation was fast approaching.

"Not into it, Wyn?" Julie asked, snuggling in the arms of Corbin, who had also passed on the drinks.

"Something like that."

Red pulled out a Baggie of dried leaves. "Cannabis, anyone? You wouldn't mind if we enjoyed this party, would you, Mr. Quick Lube?"

"*That's* more than I can handle," I glared at Donny. I had never ventured past a half glass of wine at holiday meals and had no desire to try anything that required lighting or shooting. I mostly kept my opinions to myself but was confident that the numbing qualities of his pastime contributed to Donny's absolute lack of motivation.

"Leave it," Donny pierced. Donny had a way of picking up junkies like flies on tack paper.

"It was my contribution," Red responded.

Victor began to pour another round, dripping tequila on my carpet.

"I'm done." I put my hand over the shot glass, as Victor spilled on my hand.

"One more." He was aggressive, almost bullying.

Wyn became inflamed. "She said she's done!"

Victor smashed the bottle on the table. "You're really becoming a killjoy, Mr. Castrol." Victor stood with the bottle still in his hand.

Wyn shoved him back into the wall and he stumbled to the floor, knocking down a framed photo of my father and me on Schweitzer Mountain. The glass shattered. "She said she was done."

"Wyn!" I pleaded, although I couldn't really see what was happening as my head was spinning.

Donny offered a hand to Victor, who was too sloshed to get up. Donny warned Wyn, "Calm down, brother."

Victor stood up with Donny's help, brushed past Wyn to the couch, and reached for the tequila bottle. "I think a little drop would do you good."

Wyn picked up a shard of glass, feeling it in his hand. He looked at Victor and then placed the glass on the end table, before walking out.

"Everyone sit!" Julie appeared from the kitchen holding a cake with stubs for candles sitting in pools of blue wax. Glaring at the remaining men, she said, "Happy birthday, Mags. Blow 'em out quick, before this thing melts." Julie always knew how to save a moment.

I looked at the nineteen blurred candles melting blue wax on the yellow spray-painted frosting, adorned with confetti and plastic supermarket balloon decor. This was definitely not the way I wanted to start out the new chapter in my life, drunk, artificial, and riddled with conflict. I blew out the candles, as Donny shoved a bag in my hand.

"It's a gift." I slowly looked in the bag, not sure if I should trust its contents. In the bag was a book, *The 1000 Best Dear Abby's*. My mom and I had a running joke that Dear Abby columns were for people who had absolutely no God-given common sense. It was the perfect gift, given the occasion. I hugged Donny and whispered in his ear, "You're not so bad, Cuz', at least not all the time."

"The gift is from your mom."

As Julie handed out cake, I grabbed her by the wrist and whispered, "I need to talk to you. My head is spinning--"

"Tequila does that!" Julie announced way too loudly.

"Can you help me evacuate this place?" I nodded toward Donny and company.

"On it." Julie made her way around the room, grabbing plates, some still with cake left. "It's time for me to steal the birthday girl away for some girl time. Everybody out!" She walked to the door, opened it, and herded the boys out like cattle.

Corbin hugged Julie from behind, whispering audibly in her ear, "We have practice in the morning, Jules."

Knowing that they have a ninety-minute drive ahead, I hid my disappointment. "It's not a big deal. We'll catch up later."

I watched them leave and, after shutting all the chaos out of my loft, realized that my stomach was wrenching. I filled a glass of water, but it was too late. I barely made it to the toilet to heave up tequila and birthday cake. *Happy birthday to me.* I rinsed out my mouth and its acidic aftertaste and crawled into bed, fully dressed. My vision was a blur, and my stomach was still sloshing. I tried to recall what happened with John Doe and how the big lie took place. I wanted to plan my options to resolve it. *It was such a terrible, traumatic mistake,*

I could explain. But was it? I found myself romanticizing John Doe--Jack. I don't remember at what moment my head hit the pillow.

My dreams were frantic that night. I was running Tubbs Hill, with vines and roots of trees coming to life, trying to tangle me up, like octopus tendrils. The forest was growing in on me. I ran faster, and ahead of me was Jack, by a few paces. I can't quite make him out, but I know it's him because of the bandages covering his head. As he runs, he looks back, reaching for me. A root wraps around my foot and I fall. Sirens scream at me, piercing through my brain, a cacophonic piercing-- unbearable.

My alarm is blasting, and I jolt out of bed. My throat is glue. I can hardly swallow. I sit up, my head pounding, and I steady myself, walking slowly toward the kitchen to grab a couple aspirin. After washing them down with water, I decide to start today right. I must embrace my normal routine, hungover or not.

Digging through my dresser, I find a clean pair of shorts and tee shirt, and lace up my trail shoes as steadily as I can. I hold tight to the stair rail and creak down the wooden steps to the outside.

I ran. For the entire four miles, I thought about Jack. Any moment, the usual clarity would come as the endorphin high kicks in. Nothing. My mind was blank. Nothing told me to quit the lie. Nothing told me to continue. My instincts, which I always trusted, were scrambled. I passed a runner in the opposing direction, and he startled me. I made a mental note to bring my phone with me in the future. I picked up the pace, striding all the way back to the loft. At least my adrenaline was working.

"Nothing. I'll do nothing," I confirmed aloud as I worked the key into my outside door. I rationalized that since nothing came to me, my clearest answer was to not act, hoping that my encounter with John Doe would all go away. "Sorry, Jack, but I'm breaking up with you."

"Breaking up?" a familiar voice caught me from behind.

Startled, I jumped and fell into the door. Wyn, dressed in his dark blues, held a small bouquet of flowers. "Geez, Wyn," I said.

"I brought you these, for last night. Sorry about losing my cool."

I forgot about the broken frame, my favorite picture of Dad and me on the best skiing trip ever. "You didn't have to . . ." I stopped myself. "Thank you."

"Who's the unlucky guy?" Wyn asked.

"What?" I had forgotten my pep talk.

"You were just saying you were breaking up with someone."

Caught off guard, I didn't respond.

"I guess it's none of my business," he said.

"Yeah," was all I could say.

"You run a lot, by yourself?"

"Are you writing a biography?" I could feel myself becoming impatient, overlapping my insecurity.

"You have heard about the vagrants camping out?" Wyn said.

"Yes, and I already have a father."

Wyn looked right into my eyes, the same intensity I noticed last night.

"I'll be fine," I assured him. I noticed the fragile flowers he had given me. "Thanks for the flowers."

I shut the door behind me and walked up the steps, tossing them in the garbage can.

Chapter Four: Our Story

Tuesday was the slowest day for downtown business, and mid-September was guaranteed to be slow. Summer was over, snowbirds were packing up for warmer winters, and ski vacationers hadn't arrived yet. Downtown had a calm ethereal quality. All that was missing was the single tonal music of an outdoor speaker system, and one would wonder if Jesus had returned.

This silent, gray Tuesday was exactly what I needed. I could finish an entire book on a dead day like today, or hide myself in the back of the shop and start playing with wax molds. Somehow, I knew that wouldn't happen today. First, my head hurt. Second, I couldn't stop thinking about Jack. I wanted to call Julie and ask her what she thought. Mostly, I wanted to hold his hand again and see if that was him really squeezing mine. *Okay, you're on the border of obsessing now.* Obsessing was one thing that I did well, and I'm pretty sure it's an inherited trait. My Dad has chronic migraines. He says they stem from worrying too much. I nibbled on a scone, hoping it would help with my upset stomach.

I needed to create a story, one that I could believe. Every good story had an alternate perspective, one that was believable and sympathetic. I could say that I thought he was a good friend of mine, the type you kid about marrying later in life if you both end up single and, therefore, could justify the fiancé lie. Or I could explain it was a terrible mistake in identity; I could say my fiancé showed up late that night and it wasn't him in the accident.

Or I could tell the truth. I would have to admit that I wanted to be there in his loneliness--to provide a stranger with some company. I could offer to pay a fine, do community service at the hospital, or offer *something* to show that I understood the severity of lying. I know this is the answer I needed to give. I would only resort to the sympathetic "alone on my birthday" angle if absolutely necessary.

The phone rang, startling me out of my thoughts. With my head still tender, I whispered, "Whitaker Jewelry, this is Maggie."

"Margaret Whitaker?" I didn't recognize the voice. "Margaret? This is Mira, from Kootenai Medical." A surge of hot saliva streamed under my tongue as my jaw instantly clenched. I was not expecting to have to own up so quickly.

"Look, I am really sorry about what I've done," I started, but was interrupted.

"Jack had a bleed last night," Mira said. My heart dropped into my stomach. "I think you should get here as quick as you can."

"What are you saying?" Oxytocin was shooting to my brain, the hormone that triggers bonding highs in a new mother. That is what I learned in health class, and it's the only explanation I can give for why I didn't confess right then and there. Instead, I fell immediately into nurturing mode.

"The next twenty-four hours will determine everything. I called you as soon as I could. I've left a personalized pass at reception for you to pick up, and I've cleared you to visit during this crisis. I figured you'd want to be here as much as you can."

I hesitated to respond. "Margaret?" Mira said.

"Thank you." I hung up the phone. I had thought the tsunami had hit, but apparently there were aftershocks to deal with.

I did the only thing I could think to do. I closed the store for the day, taping a sign on the door, "Closed for Tuesday, September 17. Our apologies."

There were few cars in the hospital parking lot that morning. It was colder than I realized, and I forgot my coat. I really needed to talk to Julie. Julie would have known how to handle this, would have understood why I returned.

The receptionist recognized me. With a look of motherly concern, she stood up from behind the counter. "Here you go, Sweetheart." She handed me a lanyard with a clearance badge that read NEURO/ICU *special clearance, Margaret Whitaker*. I dangled it over my head and walked through the double doors, avoiding all eye contact.

Sipping coffee and filling out paperwork, Mira stood up when she saw me arrive. "Is it over," I asked, more of a statement than a question. My heart was racing.

"Yes, it's over. The danger is over, but he dodged a bullet. The doctors had to drain fluid to relieve pressure."

"Drain? What does that mean?"

"With a drill. Dr. James will explain." Mira looked just as frightened as I felt.

I thought I might be sick, again. I was never very good with blood, and the smells and sounds of the hospital were enough to make me queasy, without being bombarded with mental images of bursting blood vessels and drilling holes in human skulls. Beyond the obvious repulsion for this sterile setting, I knew it was now or never. My confession was overdue.

"Mira, I need to talk to someone, about Jack."

She reached for another brochure.

"No. I mean, I need to confess something. I did something terrible--"

"You cannot blame yourself for this. What has happened, has happened. There is no point in dwelling on the past. Trust me, that does *not* help anyone." Mira was passionate in her lecture, tension swelling in her voice.

"Even if I told you I'm not the girl you think I am?" *There. I said it.* She was going to escort me out, if not throw me out.

"You need a grief counselor who's trained to handle these kinds of emotions." Mira began to fumble around at her station, and then found a stack of brochures and gave one to me. "Look. I see this all the time. I don't care who you are or what guilt you're dealing with. Don't leave him now. That's just wrong."

Mira pulled me by the elbow into Jack's room. Dr. James was standing bedside, charting numbers off an ultrasound readout. He smiled when he saw me.

"He's looking a lot better this morning," he said. "The swelling is decreasing, slowly."

Jack's bandage was rearranged, now securing his forehead and the back of his skull, showing his lower face for the first time. A large pad of gauze was taped behind his temple, where a tube came out of his skull. His black eyelashes were now

50

joined with bushy black eyebrows, and dark overgrown stubble covered his jaw and neck. His black hairline was shaved, unevenly; an obvious rush job necessary for emergency surgery. I stared in silence, yet wanted to scream, *I'm not his fiancé! I'm an imposter!* But the fragility of the situation demanded silence.

"Come here, Margaret." The doctor pulled a chair next to Jack's bed, and I sat down. "Let him know you're here." The doctor placed my hand on his hand. "Don't be afraid. Talk to him, remind him your name. Remind him all about you. We won't know how much cognition he will have if . . . *when* he wakes up, but it may comfort him now."

Sitting next to him, I gently felt his rough, large hands. They were swollen and chaffed, and his fingernails were cracked.

"I'll let you spend some time alone," Dr. James said. "If he shows any sign of discomfort, just push the emergency button."

A need to care for Jack was infecting me. Mira looked on, watching me near this delicate life.

Dr. James left first, and Mira followed. I was all alone with Jack, staring at his jagged face, until my visceral bonding was distracted by Dr. James and Mira whispering outside the door. I slowly tiptoed to the door and shut it.

Returning to his bedside, I stared at him for several minutes, deafening silence filling the room. "It's me again, Maggie. I'm glad you made it. You're defying the odds, if you want to know the truth." I looked at him, so peaceful. I was aware of the constant beeping in the room. "That speaks well for you. You're a fighter." I looked down at my hand which was resting on his. My hands were calloused from working in the shop, desperately in need of some moisturizer. His hands were swollen and, for the most part, clean. His fingernails were freshly clipped, but I noticed dirt hidden between the web of his fingers. Seized with an idea, I stood up and began rummaging under cupboards and drawers until I found a washcloth. I dampened the cloth in the sink with warm water and began to clean his hands.

"Echk-hem!" Mira cleared her throat. "What are you doing?"

Either my heart stopped beating, or my blood stopped circulating. Moments ago I was begging to reveal my secret. Now I wanted to protect it.

"A little dirt. I wanted to--"

"Here." Mira pulled out a towel and plastic basin from a closet next to the sink. "I've bathed him every day, but he needs extra work." She set up a washing station on a moving cart and rolled it next to me. "He's got a dirty day job." She put on medical gloves and handed me a pair. I hesitated, not sure if she was asking a question. I dried my hands on my sweater and put on the gloves. I smiled at her and nodded, which was enough to dodge her question.

"So, what's your story?" Mira placed a washcloth in the tub of warm water and rung it dry. "He's a lot older than you. Obviously, you didn't meet in school." She began to clean one hand.

I picked up the other and washed between each finger, while creating our history. "I was on my way to San Diego--senior trip with a few friends--and our flight was packed. There weren't enough seats to all sit together, so we had to split up. I sat next to Jack, who was in the center, with an elderly lady next to the window. Jack and this woman strike up an endless conversation about her deceased husband and how her kids live all over the U.S. and she is all alone--the entire flight. It was torturous, to sit next to this gorgeous man and not have one single opportunity to flirt. When our plane landed in L.A. for a layover, I exited among the masses for a quick restroom break, only to have Jack whisper from behind, 'I'll buy you a drink to make up for it.' When I told him that I wasn't staying in L.A., just getting off to stretch before my last leg to San Diego, he insisted one airport drink wouldn't cause delay. Long story short, I missed the plane, and Jack drove me to San Diego, sunset included."

I massaged the washcloth up his arm, pulling his gown up to his biceps. His arms were strong, yet fragile.

"You're lying!" Mira said, mesmerized. "There is no way that happens in real life."

I looked at Mira, and I could tell she believed the story. I rinsed off the washcloth and washed his scruffy neckline. "The best part--he didn't ask for my number. He didn't say, 'I'll call you.'"

"What did he say?"

"He said, 'I'm pretty positive that you are not a coincidence.'"

"No!"

"And"--I was creating our story so fast that even I was excited about it--"and I don't think I'll ever--*could ever*-- live my life not knowing what happened to passenger 14A."

"Get out!" Mira was now washing Jack's neck, staring at him. "I didn't peg him for that type."

As I worked my way up to his cheeks, I saw a crust of dried blood below his ear. His black stubble was rough on the washcloth. I rinsed again, turning the tub cloudy red. I took the tub to the sink, pouring it out to refill it with fresh water.

"My father always told me that a man should chase you, go to the ends of the earth for you, prove to you he means business; anything less, and he's not worth it. So I told Jack, 'Margaret Claire Whitaker, Coeur d'Alene, Idaho. There's only one of me in town.'"

"Good move." Mira said.

"And seven days later when I returned from San Diego, I found a bouquet of red roses at my apartment, with a note from Jackson Darren. Two weeks later he visited, and the rest is history."

Mira froze, lost in her thoughts. She looked at me and then back at Jack, and let out a long sigh.

Jack was rugged and mysterious, maybe even homeless. I didn't care. He had a story. *We* had a story. I moistened the cloth in the clean water, and I asked Mira, "Is it okay, his face--"

"You can wash his face. Just be gentle."

I blotted his eyes as softly as I could. His eyelids were tired and worn. I nudged at his nose. He had a sweet nose, in contrast to his weathered skin.

Mira had since left his side, and before leaving the room, bent down to me and whispered, "You have a beautiful story."

****

Ever since I developed *our story* and shared it with Mira, I became more and more addicted to filling in the timeline of our life together. It was a game, a time filler, an obsession. Thinking of a past and present life with him, fictional as it was, was much more exciting than succumbing to the reality that I was living a pretty ho-hum life.

I developed a routine that worked well for running the shop and visiting Jack daily. After my morning run, I would close the shop at 4 p.m. to eat dinner with Jack, next to him, every night while he slept. I talked to him about the jewelry shop, the oddity in the customers who came in, and often revealed my relationship predictions. He was the most patient of listeners.

"This man came in today, Mr. Wheeler, Bob Wheeler, President of Silver Bank of North Idaho, and wanted a solitaire pendant on a sixteen-inch chain. His wife already has a solitaire that I designed for her two years back. Now, Mr. Wheeler isn't very sensitive to his wife. She's sort of demanding, if you know what I mean. She usually has to approve every purchase he makes. So when he came in to make an order, I was naturally suspicious." Jack slept peacefully. "I think he's got a fling on the side. Mrs. Wheeler is going to kill him if she finds out. Not if, *when*. She will find out."

I started to fidget with my finger. "I just finished a new design, and I brought it to show you." I took the simple band of quarter-carat diamonds, shaped like an eternity ring, off my left hand ring finger and held it up to Jack. "I haven't named it yet, but I'm thinking it will be something to do with you." I slipped it back on, admiring it. I liked the way it felt, smooth and simple.

Yawning, I realized it was nine o'clock at night. I pulled up his sterile, crisp bedsheets and tucked him in. Then I did something that somewhat shocked me--I kissed his forehead. "Good night." I left the room, my heart fluttering.

The mornings were getting dark and cold. Fall seemed to switch like a light in North Idaho. One day it's seventy and sunny, and the next it is forty-five and drizzly. Regardless of the temperature, I always started the day with a run on Tubbs Hill.

As I came down the steps of the loft and opened the door to darkness, a shadow stepped out in front of me. I burst out, "Get back!"

"It's me, Maggie." Wyn had his hands up in the air, holding a blunt object in one hand.

"Geez, Wyn, are you making a habit of freaking me out?" My heart was out of sync with its beating.

"I brought you something," he said.

"You don't have to keep doing this. I've forgiven you already."

"Bear spray." Wyn handed me a black tube with a red warning label. "It's got a clip on it that you can tuck in your vest, for when you run."

"Because of bears on Tubbs Hill?" Everyone knew that Tubbs Hill was surrounded by the city. Maybe an occasional deer or opossum will visit, but bears, impossible.

"Because of the bums." Wyn looked at me with a nervous tension, the third time I noticed the intensity in his eyes. "Listen, Whitaker. There are some really scary people in this world."

"I thought they all lived in Alaska." I wasn't going to accept his patronizing overprotection easily. Plus, it was fun to make fun of his stint with baseball in Alaska.

"Yeah, but some of them move back." Wyn's eyes bulged, and then he winked. He could take a joke.

"If you want to know the truth, Donny gave us each twenty-five dollars for your party, and I don't feel right about keeping it. I thought it was more apropos to re-gift it."

"Thanks, I guess," I said, more sarcastic than grateful.

"You know, Tubbs is getting icy, and dark. You really think you ought to be running this early?"

"I'm a much nicer person if I get that morning endorphin kick." I noticed that Wyn was wearing jogging attire. "Do you have some protective order from my father or something?"

Just as I had suspected, Wyn started walking towards the trailhead with me.

"Just instinct."

"Instinct? What does that mean?" I could feel my blood boiling.

"You're small, pretty, and completely overconfident that nothing bad will ever happen to you."

I knew Wyn was trying to compliment me, but for some reason he was pissing me off. I was never a believer in doom and gloom, not for my life at least.

"I'll take the bear spray, to ease your mind." I grabbed it from his hands, and then started jogging. I held it up and yelled back, "I feel much safer now." But before I was ten strides, Wyn caught up to me, running. "Go away, Wyn."

"I've always wanted to become a runner."

I was now insulted. "Don't slow me down," I threatened, and increased my pace intentionally.

The run was crisp, fast, and frantic. The trail narrowed to a single runner's width. I jetted ahead, with Wyn on my heels. The sun was breaking over the water like a gorgeous painting, but at this pace, I didn't have time to enjoy it. I raced around the back side of Tubbs on the second loop, ending the four miles in a full sprint. Two strides behind, Wyn was barely able to catch his breath, just as I had hoped. This would show him. *Who needs bear spray, or Wyn?*

He caught his breath while holding his hands on his side. I walked in circles to catch my own breath. We didn't speak a word to each other. Despite my resistance, I had to admit a tiny enjoyment of crushing Wyn, and watching him take it like a man. It surprised me, how his protective nature was annoying yet comforting.

We walked to the back alley of my loft in silence. He finally spoke when I reached my door. "Tell me this wasn't your normal pace."

"It was a quick tempo." Humbling Wyn became an enjoyable game. "I'm pretty confident that I could outrun any bum on the hill."

"Yeah," he confessed between pants.

Chapter Five: Pressure

"**W**e're all going out tonight," Donny mentioned as he peaked his head in the front door of Whitaker Jewelry. "Wyn wanted me to *mention* it to you."

"I've got plans." I said, my head buried under a glass case, cleaning the glass in the far reaches with a paper towel.

"Your mom and dad are not due home for three more weeks. You can't possibly have plans." Donny liked to insult me as much as he could.

"Whatever you say, Donny."

"You seeing someone?" he asked.

"Privileged information."

Donny stepped all the way into the store. "You're wearing a ring. And there's nobody here. Did your imaginary friend come back?"

I had completely forgotten that I was wearing *Jack London*, the new setting I wore to the hospital last night. The ring was cold and pure as ice, and tied in perfectly with the new Jack in my life. "This is a new Lenora original, for your information." Donny looked uninterested, forging a nod. A customer came in the store. "If you'll excuse me," I said with a smirk on my face, "I've got work to do."

Donny scooted closer to me, now whispering, "We'll be at the dock at nine, if by chance your *plans don't materialize.*" He was about to leave, and then asked, "Online, maybe?" And then he thought better of it, "Nah, spare me the details." He left, and I noticed Victor and Red waiting outside for him.

The day dragged slowly by, and I couldn't focus on anything but Jack. I considered myself his guardian angel, fitted to do a job until he no longer needed me. Although his rugged hands, neck, and jaw proved him to be at one point strong, he lay there in a catatonic, helpless way, day after day. I longed for his presence. Every thought or desire conjured an image of his resting face. The only way I could take my mind off of Jack was to read. I picked up an old copy of *The Good Earth* from Dad's bookshelf in his office, helping to make the anticipated four-o'clock hour roll around more quickly. I locked up the store, turned the "CLOSED" sign facing out, and jetted to my dinner date.

Mira was waiting at the nurses' station, a shimmer in her eyes.

"Everything okay?" I asked.

Mira could hardly contain herself. "Dr. James said that Jack's afternoon ultrasound looks great, the clot has gone down enough to attempt to wake him."

The news stopped me in my tracks, inducing a sudden wave of nausea. "Wake him? Now?" This wasn't good news. This was terrible.

"If he passes the pressure test." Mira's smile was blinding.

"Pressure test?" My smile was not.

Dr. James arrived, taking me gently by the elbow. "Walk in with me. I'd like to have a word with you." Dr. James led me inside room 331. Mira followed.

In Jack's room was an older gentleman. Dr. James introduced him. "This is Dr. Easton who works neurosurgery and recovery at the rehabilitation center across town. We like to work on this critical phase in teams." He was an older man, compassionate by nature, yet all science.

"Jack's doing real well," Dr. Easton spoke calmly. "The hematoma two nights ago was not atypical, and we were prepared for it. We will not know if the initial trauma, or the recent bleed, has caused any brain damage until we wake him, if we can."

"We're going to perform a pressure test now, after I double-check his clot," Dr. James said, while running an ultrasound probe across his skull. "You can hold his hand during this test." Dr. James started to talk to himself while looking at the ultrasound screen. "Yes, everything looks good to go. I like the look of that." Then Dr. James informed me of the proceeding test, while Dr. Easton gathered the bulbous syringe at the end of tubing attached to a machine. He put the syringe close to Jack's ear. "We'll administer a quick jolt of cold air into the ear canal. He won't feel it, but Jack's reaction determines a lot. He may flinch, yelp, any number of things."

My stomach was swirling like a funnel cloud.

Mira scooted the visitor's chair right next to the bed, and I timidly sat down. I wish I could get my body to stop shaking. *Control your hands. Don't let them see you shaking.* "Excuse me," I apologized. "I'm sorry." I stood up and walked away. I stopped steps before the door, inhaling a calming breath.

Mira took my place at Jack's bedside and held his hand, stroking it gently. Dr. James and Dr.

Easton both fixated an instrument to Jack's inner ear, one holding it in place, the other bracing his head. Dr. James slowly counted aloud, "Three, two, one."

A small squeeze of a nozzle, a quick burst of air, and Jack let out a yelp, a piercing cry that penetrated through the hallways.

I shuddered. I slowly turned to look at Jack, attended by the two doctors and a nurse. Mira's hands reached toward Jack's face, her index finger gently sliding his lips shut again.

The doctors started charting, fidgeting with machines, looking at graph paper. Mira exhaled, the corners of her lips gradually revealing the evolving smile that burst forth.

"Margaret," Dr. James said, "that is the sound of life. Jack has, at some level, brain function. To what extent is to be determined. We can now wake him up."

I stared at the wall, nauseated.

"His last dose of Propofol was administered four hours ago. I'd say another hour and he may start to stir," Dr. James said.

"An hour," I repeated. It was imminent that this day would come. I just didn't want it to come so soon.

Dr. James and Dr. Easton both left the room. They mumbled something to Mira on their way out, something about paging them when he starts responding. An hour. My stomach moans broke my concentration. I wandered down to the cafeteria to get a tray of food. I had grown oddly fond of eating on a tray, but more accurately fond of my dinner dates with Jack. This was the last supper.

After filling my cafeteria tray with beef stroganoff, peas, and the homemade roll I looked forward to nightly, I made the slow journey back to Jack's room. On the way, I noticed the staff buzz around me, just another day at the office.

I took my tray into Jack's room and ate bedside, in silence. I picked at the roll, twisting it into tiny morsels and making a pile on my tray. I placed my hand on his fingers, the diamond engagement ring glistening under the fluorescent hospital lights. Softly, his fingertips moved in my hand.

Mira stepped into the room. "I don't mean to interrupt." She stood at the door. "If you see any sign of him waking up, twitching, anything--please call. Push the red button."

I looked at Mira and nodded. She smiled and walked out.

Jack's hands flinched, as did his shoulders. Nausea was overtaking me. I shut my eyes, hoping that I wouldn't see his open before I could get away. With my head down, I turned my back on him. I raced down the hallway and barely made it out the hospital doors before I vomited in the nearest bush.

I sat in my car in the parking lot, my head still spinning. I pulled out my cell phone, autodialing number three.

A voicemail recording sounded: "It's Julie. Spill the drama, and I'll call you back--BEEP."

"Jules, I'm driving over to Moscow to see you. I'll be there in an hour and a half."

The drive through the Palouse--miles and miles of rolling farmlands--gave me time to clear my head. Jack was probably fluttering his eyes open now. I wondered what color his eyes were, brown or blue? I thought about his gentle nose, contrasting his strong jaw and thick neck. I had known every part of his frail body: his ears, his forehead, his hands. I loved holding his hands.

I missed him. I must be insane, I told myself, giving myself a mental lecture. Attachment syndrome is common in any caretaking field. Counselors have to learn to separate their emotions from their job. Oncologists have to separate the sadness of dealing with cancer's torturous toll, so they can live their own healthy life. I didn't realize detaching would be so hard.

Ninety minutes felt like a second, and suddenly I was driving past the main gate of the University of Idaho. I looked for the tall tower, Theophilus, the dorm I helped haul boxes and boxes up to floor four to Julie's new room.

Theo Tower wasn't difficult to spot, with the red brick jetting up above the surrounding Spruce and Pine Trees. Inside the lobby, students played keep-away soccer, with girls pushing boys over furniture and knocking a recycle soda container sideways. I walked around the mayhem. I felt like a foreigner, on a campus that I had no part of.

In the stairwell was a droopy-faced underclassman huddled closely with a girl, their hands intertwined. My presence was an intrusion. They sat in silence and waited for me to pass by. I climbed to the fourth floor and entered the hallway. A girl in a bathrobe with wet hair twisted in a turban walked barefoot out of the common bathroom. It seemed odd to me, communal living. I walked to Julie's room at the end of the hall.

On her door was a glittered plaque stating JULIE and next to it KAREN. There was a picture of Julie and Karen, smiling together. Adjacent to the door hung a dry erase board with the phrase "Karen and Julie rock!" written in scrawled handwriting.

I knocked, and thought I heard a scuffle in the room. Nobody came to the door. I knocked again. The door slightly cracked open.

"What?" I heard Julie question. Julie squinted, her eyes not adjusting to the fluorescent lights of the hall. "Maggie?"

"You didn't get my message?" I asked.

"I didn't check," Julie admitted, opening the door further. "Everything okay?" She looked back into her room, and then opened the door wider. Corbin was sitting on her bed, both he and Julie wearing Vandal workout clothes. "Come in," Julie offered.

"Oh, geez, I'm interrupting. I can come back," I said.

"We were just taking a nap." Julie said.

Corbin slid past me. "I gotta go." Julie kissed him goodbye. He acknowledged me, "Maggie."

I turned to Julie in complete shock. "This is awkward." I fumbled an apology.

Julie grabbed me by the elbow. "We were taking a nap. Honestly, its fine." Julie continued, "I have a class at 8 a.m. one day, at 6 p.m. the next. My schedule is all over the board. And with running--I nap a lot."

"You and Corbin . . . it's serious?"

"I like him. A lot." Julie's eyes sparkled like a little girl's.

"He seems great. I'm surprised a little. You've always been noncommittal."

"I know," she admitted. "This is different though. He's actually a good guy. It's not just for fun. It's . . . real." Julie stopped herself and looked at me. "I should not be talking about me. What is going on with you?" I looked at Julie and sat silently. Words evaded me. "What's going on, Maggie?"

Again, I stared at her, until a sudden silliness came over me, and I laughed.

"Is this a guy thing?" Julie asked.

"Yes." I admitted.

"Fun." Julie was getting silly.

"Not fun." I composed myself.

"Drama." We were playing charades, and Julie misread my lead.

"Julie, I'm in a . . . dilemma."

"A dilemma." Julie transformed her excited demeanor into complete gravity. With a hypnotic, deep, resounding solemnity, she sat on the floor, criss-crossed her legs, and invited me to do the same. "Sit."

"You cannot repeat one ounce of this to a living soul," I said while sitting.

"What's his name?" she prodded.

"Jack."

"How did you meet?"

"The paper." I said.

Julie's eyes bulged. "The paper? Who does that anymore?"

"Not like that. He was in the local news, the subject of a story I've been following."

"A local story." Julie was following me so far.

"And so I met him."

"Okay. This is interesting," Julie admitted.

"And he's not totally comprehensive of our relationship, our relationship which I manufactured."

Julie's face shriveled up in confusion. In one big, long run-on breath, I confessed: "He was in an

66

accident--a John Doe--and critical, maybe even dying, and I went to the hospital to see him, just to comfort him since the paper kept reporting that he was all alone with no identity; and it was nice, to sit with him, every day, and the only way I could keep seeing him was to say that I was engaged to him." I twirled the Jack London ring around my finger. I stared at the floor for a moment, until I was able to meet Julie's gaze, hoping to find any semblance of understanding. All I noticed was her chin on the floor.

"You're engaged to a man in a coma?" She was putting the pieces together. "Is he still in a coma?"

"That's my second dilemma." I looked at Julie through insecure eyes.

"He's not in a coma." Julie was getting hotter.

"They're waking him, right now," I said.

"And he doesn't know about you?" My look answered her question.

I decided to tell her the whole story, from the moment I had my birthday dinner at Chinese Gardens and witnessed the love between the couple on the bench, to the newspaper revealing that John Doe was in the hospital alone, to when I attempted to tell Mira that I wasn't his fiancé and she berated me for leaving. "He started improving once I showed up. Everyone says so, and so now I feel obligated to him."

"You're chasing. We don't chase. It's an inversion of power." Julie said.

"I wasn't chasing. I was just helping. I didn't think he'd *live*."

Julie was flabbergasted. "You are the most normal of all my friends. And yet, this is *not* normal. Going to college is *normal*. Spending every waking moment with your college boyfriend is *normal.* But making up phony relationships, false engagements, with men that you don't know in the guise of "helping them" is *not* normal. It's deranged."

I sat, punched in the gut, her words ringing very true.

"Look, I know your heart. You love to love. You love to help. But you can't save everybody. You have to read a sad story, and just let it be sad."

I knew she was right, and I was ashamed. "What do I do now?" I asked, hoping she'd have the one magical answer that would make this all go away.

"Nothing. You do nothing."

"What about the hospital staff, all the people who are expecting me to be with Jack?"

"Just walk away. I'm sure you wouldn't be the first." She said it with such detached emotion. "Mags, look at me." I saw fear in her eyes. "Do *not* go to the hospital. This is not your charity case. You made a mistake, and you are going to undo that mistake, by staying away."

Julie stood up, walked across the room, and opened her dresser. She tossed a pair of sweats at me. "You're staying with me tonight. It's time to be nineteen again."

We heard a faint commotion outside, which slowly grew louder and louder. Julie threw herself across the room and opened her dorm window. Girls were draping themselves out of each window, sneaking a peak at a band of fifty freshmen running naked in formation, solely with sneakers on and each hosting a bandana over their face while singing some undetectable university chant. Girls whistled and hollered, and one threw a red laced bra down onto the streakers.

I lie at the foot of her twin bed, my feet near her head and vice versa. As I drifted off to sleep thinking of the freshmen initiation I was privy to, I asked, "Where's your roommate?"

"Karen will be in later, much later," Julie answered.

Karen did sneak in, at about 2 a.m. I thought I heard a scuffle at some point in the night, but I never fully gained consciousness. My body had completely let down and I was out.

I heard a knock just before 8 a.m. I sat up to find Julie towel drying her hair, in fresh clothes, with Corbin standing in the doorway with his books. Julie grabbed a textbook off her desk and cradled it. "Morning, Mags. I'll be in class for the next two hours. Stay as long as you like."

I couldn't believe I overslept. I was letting Dad down with the mismanagement of the shop. Julie's reprimand to me was exactly what I needed.

"You're going back." Julie looked panicked.

"I'm going back to the shop, to work."

"Remember, normal--nineteen." Julie left with Corbin. They made a cute pair, I decided.

I found my car keys. Karen shuffled in her bed, pulling the covers farther over her body. I left the room, still not ever meeting her, not even seeing her face.

It poured buckets during the drive back to Coeur d'Alene. My windshield wipers couldn't clear the water fast enough. The beeping of my phone let me know that I had an unattended voice message--five, actually. I listened to them on speakerphone.

Donny called first, wanting me to join him at the dock last night, per Wyn's request.

The next two messages were from Wyn himself. The first was at 6:10 a.m. He was wondering if I was planning on running. He didn't want to wake me by ringing my doorbell. The second was Wyn calling to see if I was alive. He said that he felt odd about me not showing up for my run, and then noticed the store was still closed on his way to work.

The fourth call was from my dad, reporting from France. They were having a phenomenal time. I felt ashamed, hearing my dad's voice. I know he loves me unconditionally, but it would be unbearable for Dad to know what has transpired.

Finally, it was Wyn, again, worried. He was on a five-minute break and needed to know I was okay. He asked me to please call him and left his number. I turned off the phone and threw it on the console.

By the time I unlocked the front door to the shop and turned the CLOSED sign to OPEN, it was nearly noon. I picked up the *North Idaho Press* from the mail slot, afraid to look at the headlines. In an attempt to take Julie's advice, I tossed the paper in the trash can, still inside its protective plastic. I couldn't read about him anymore. The answering machine was blinking red, announcing messages left. I unlocked the metal grates over the jewelry, disarmed the store, and pushed that pulsating red button.

First message: Mira, trying to locate me as Jack was waking up.

Second message: Mira, trying to locate me as Jack was now awake and coherent.

Third message: Mira, informing that Jack had asked for me.

Impossible. This was a trick.

I pulled the morning's newspaper out of the trash can and searched it for clues that the hospital had discovered my fraud. I found nothing regarding John Doe. For a brief moment, I contemplated calling Mira back to tell her I was walking away. But my record of actually doing that was pretty bad. I needed to stay away. I needed to stay busy. I grabbed a polishing cloth and began to buff jewelry. *Jack London* still sat on my finger. I took him off, cleaned him up, and found a place under the glass to showcase him.

The front bell jingled. A young couple entered.

"Welcome," I said. The couple was nice enough, just window shopping, and moseyed around the glass cases, enjoying each other's company.

"I'll be in the back," I announced, as I ducked into the studio. With this much in my head, I need to channel this energy and create. I wasn't inspired in my usual way. No men of valor, greatness, or heroics impressed upon me today. I was inspired by a little girl, Poor Fool, from The Good Earth. Her father loved her, despite her being a female and of limited mind. She was the only one who wasn't a threat to him and the only one he could trust to love. I took out my sketch pad and scrawled a simple sweeping band with a flat, etched surface. I wrote POOR FOOL under it. I left an oval for the jewel to be buried, maybe not even a diamond, but a pearl- like a piece of rice- dull and soft.

The front door bell jingled. The young couple must have stepped out. I am alone now, able to get lost in wax molding. Yes, that's what I'd do. I had to stop thinking about Jack. What did Mira mean exactly when she said he asked for me? Was it possible that he actually heard the stories I had told him?

I traced Poor Fool in wax paper. With an X-Acto blade, I sliced off a quarter-inch thick circle of wax. With a metal tool, I etched in every curve, every notch, and every indentation. The wax was nearly a perfected mold, completed in nearly minutes. I left a big, gaping void in the center of the wax, to eventually place the stone.

Working under a light, steadying the wax mold in my fingers, I fine-tuned the details with a sharp blade. Movement by the back office door caught my eye. Wyn was leaning against the door frame, watching me.

"She lives." It was matter-of-fact, an observation.

"I was out last night." I focused on the mold more intently.

Wyn put his hands in his pockets and kicked at his feet. "Donny told me you're seeing someone?"

"Don't believe everything Donny says." The mention of Donny made me short.

"Well, you're alive. Mission accomplished." Wyn turned his back on me, about to leave, when he added, "I waited an hour this morning. I thought maybe I'd join you."

I was hoping it wasn't going to come to this. Some people don't do subtlety. "Wyn, you've been really kind to me lately. I don't exactly know why, but I can guess. I think you should know I'm sort of *involved* right now."

Wyn nodded. "He's good to you?" Wyn shifted his weight back and forth. I didn't respond. "Sorry. It's none of my business." Yet he dared to continue. "You look different, that's all, like you're hiding something. You can tell me if he's . . . well, you can tell me anything."

I am the one who hasn't been good. I've been manipulative, sneaky, and to quote Julie, *deranged.* I needed to change the subject. "Are they overstaffed at the Quick Lube today?"

Wyn got the point loud and clear yet took it like a gentleman. "I've got the afternoon off. I've got a mechanic's exam tomorrow."

His gentle response to my hostility made me feel like a jerk. I could be a *little nicer,* I thought. Wyn was, in some aspects, a perfect distraction. "Do you need a study partner?" I asked out of the blue.

"A tutor?" Wyn said and smiled. "That's okay. You don't need to--"

"I'd love to." It was time to start being nineteen again.

He was taken aback at the sudden change of my attitude. "Okay, I guess," Wyn said. "You want to meet at the library after dinner?"

"We can meet upstairs in the loft. I'll order pizza." I was overeager.

"Kind of a boring date, pizza and studying."

"Not a date, just a distraction . . . from him." Wyn suppressed a smile.

"I'm not going to get beat up or anything?" he smirked.

"I highly doubt it." I said.

The phone rang. "Whitaker Jewelry, Margaret speaking." It was her again, bringing me back to the one place I wanted to forget.

"Margaret, it's Mira. Everyone's worried about you, and I've assured the staff that the police don't need to get involved. I know this is hard--everyone deals with trauma differently--but please come see him. I can arrange to have a social worker help you through it."

"I can't see him. I can't," I whispered into the phone.

"He's asking for you. You're all he asks for."

"He's better off without me." I hung up the phone, abruptly.

Wyn, whose eyes wandered to the contents of the studio, tried to play it cool, seeing I was visually shaken. "You okay?" he asked.

"I have to be." I put the wax molding away in a wooden box, repositioned all the appliances, and shut off the studio lights. "Wyn, will you wait with me?"

Wyn stood there, concerned, waiting for any indication that I would share my burden with him. I managed to avoid him by securing the metal grids over the jewelry cases, gathering my belongings, activating the security alarms, and locking the front door.

Wyn walked with me around the building and through the muddy parking lot to the back door. I keyed myself in and insisted, "Come on up. Please. We can study. Right now would be perfect."

"Man, this guy really messed you up. Do me a favor. Point him out to me, and I'll mess *him* up."

"Can we please not talk about him, *at all*?" I was feeling protective of Jack, wishing I could just explain to Wyn that Jack's not the problem.

Wyn didn't say anything, although I could tell he felt threatened.

"It's over now, so that's all that matters," I confessed.

"Good, cuz' I don't like this guy already." I chose to drop it, for Wyn's sake and mine. I picked up the phone and called King Pizza, ordering a veggie thin crust. Wyn stared at the photo of Dad and me, hung back on the wall, sans the glass. "Veg?" he complained.

"You'll thank me in the morning. Running on a cowboy pizza is never a good idea."

"So we're back on?" Wyn asked.

"My life is going to resume its normal routine, starting now. And I could use a running partner." Maybe I was being selfish, but I needed the company, with Dad out of the shop for three more weeks and Julie in college. "Don't get ahead of yourself, Wyn. Where's your book? Don't you have a text or something that I can quiz you on?"

"It's in my truck," he said.

"Do you want to go get it?"

Wyn looked at me and smiled. "I've read it once. I'll pass."

"You don't retain everything you read just once," I said.

I've got a good memory." Wyn smiled, again.

I could feel the confidence in his reply. He wasn't worried at all. "Why aren't you in college?" I never pegged Wyn as the academic type, until now.

"I didn't apply," he admitted.

"Why not?"

"I wanted to play ball."

"But you quit." It seemed too simple for me to believe. "You don't just quit your dreams after one bad summer. What really happened in Alaska?" I asked.

"I didn't quit. It may look like I quit, but I didn't quit."

"If you didn't quit, why are you here?"

"The American Legion league is for college-enrolled students. When the league found out I had not applied anywhere, the manager of the team enrolled me in Anchorage Community College to ensure my summer eligibility."

"You didn't want to go there?"

"Alaska was a fun place to play summer ball. It's incredible there. But it wasn't home. I could feel it right away."

"But you're giving up baseball."

"Baseball is the greatest game on the planet, but it's not enough. The game, for the game itself, isn't enough. I was living in an apartment with three guys--great guys and all--but they were all moving on. I was the only one staying."

"Can you transfer to a college that you want to go to, to a place you like, so you can still play ball?"

"I like this place," Wyn said. "This is home."

I understood him. I knew my place too, even if everyone in my life tried to convince me to move on for a while. I knew that I was going to run the shop with Dad and eventually take over. It was my home.

"I'm glad you're here," I said. "I needed a new running partner."

The doorbell rang, and Wyn retrieved the pizza at the bottom of the steps. When he returned, I tried to offer him cash, but he wouldn't accept.

"Can I ask you something?" Wyn opened the pizza box, avoiding eye contact.

"Sure."

"What is it with older guys? Is it the money, the power . . . ?"

"How did you know he is older?"

"I didn't, until now." Wyn smiled, and then admitted, "Just a hunch. Who is he?"

I cut him off. "We agreed not to talk about him. Remember?"

"Why not? If it's over--"

"Can we not talk about it." I was a little shocked how intensely private I felt about Jack.

"Sorry. I guess I'm just a little wary of the older guy thing. You're just out of high school."

"So are you."

Wyn picked up on my sensitivity. Just like Julie, he was able to save the moment. "Whitaker, just think, if I had gone off to college, I would have always thought of you as Donny's mundane cousin."

"Mundane?" I had never considered myself that way. "How about creative, maybe a bit introverted, analytical, anti-social even, but mundane?"

Wyn cinched his shoulders up. "It was just an impression. It didn't last. What did you think of me?" Wyn looked sure of my response.

"I didn't . . . form any opinions of you."

"Nice," Wyn said.

"You're Donny's friend. Therefore I just ignored you."

"See!" Wyn pointed his finger at me. "In that statement is an impression. You thought we were not worthy of your time--a lesser-than."

"We had nothing in common. I didn't know you. You were Donny's friend."

"Why do you hate Donny?"

Because Donny pities himself, and that is something I don't do. He's a user, and he looks out for one person only. He makes friends with people so that he can get something out of them."

"Donny's friends show up for your birthday party. Donny's friends stick around." Suddenly this conversation went from somewhat playful to heated.

"Victor, Red? It never changes. Those aren't friends. They were *paid* to attend my birthday."

Wyn sat silent for a moment. "Donny's not a bad person. I hope you can see that one day." Then Wyn admitted, "He is a pretty bad roommate though."

"I can imagine. I'm going to have to send you back to that roommate now. We've got a long run in the morning."

Wyn, satiated with pizza, held his stomach. "A long run? How long is long?"

"You don't have to run with me. I have bear spray," I said. I was testing his loyalty.

"I *could* use the extra sleep before my test," Wyn added.

"Well, if sleep helps you, you should sleep." *Right back at you, Wyn.*

Wyn sat up straight. He looked right into my eyes. "Do you want me to join you Maggie, or not? No more games."

Again, I had all the power, but I felt so childish. "I like your company."

Wyn got up and grabbed the pizza box. "I'm going. I could use the extra sleep. I'll take this to the dumpster on my way out." And like that, he walked out the door. He called my bluff.

I crawled into bed and thought about Wyn's loneliness in Alaska. Wyn finished the season. He didn't quit the team midseason, but saw his commitment to completion. I had quit on Jack. I knew it was wrong for me to continue the lie, yet he was asking for me. I drifted off to sleep, picturing Jack awake, and wondered if there was any way for me to tie up all these loose ends. I could think of none.

Chapter Six: Awakened

Before the sun arose, my dreaded alarm woke me from the deepest of sleep, where no dreams could exist. It was nice to not think, not dream about anything. When I realized it was sleep, and not just a fresh start, I felt grumpy.

I dressed in warm fleece sweats, tied my running shoes, and fumbled down the steps. I half expected Wyn to stand me up, after the bad mood I left him with. I opened the door and there he was, his back to my door, looking toward the lake.

"Morning," I offered, somewhat apologetically.

Somber, he turned and looked at me, "I think we need to take to the streets. Tubbs Hill is icy. It's not safe." I don't like to be told what to do, but he was right. It's nearly impossible to run on the back side, where no light hits to defrost the ice that gathers overnight.

"We can do the Centennial Trail," I said. We walked one block to join the 56-mile paved trail that gives runners and bikers a wide path through the city all the way to Spokane. "I wasn't sure if you were going to be here this morning," I finally admitted.

Wyn was silent for a long time. "I wasn't sure either, but I don't like you out in the dark alone."

"Don't run for me," I finally said. We started running. It was easier to talk to him while running; that way I didn't have to look at his face. "I want you to run with me, but don't run for me. Can you do that?" I didn't want to lose Wyn. I had just found him.

"If that's what it takes."

"If that's what it takes for what?"

Wyn did not respond. In the silence that followed, I suspected that Wyn had an elevated view of my goodness. He had no idea that I had ditched a guy in the hospital, hoping the mess of lies would escape me. He had no idea the type of flaws I had just discovered in myself. Maybe if I could get over Jack and get out of this mess unscathed, there could be some redeeming qualities left in me. But if he found out what types of games I was really capable of, he would never want to see me again.

We ran the rest of the five miles in silence.

****

It was midweek Wednesday, another sluggish day for downtown business. I was back to routine, with a juice and red-currant-wheat-germ scone for breakfast, along with my daily paper. Consciously, I was attempting to be professional and mature, reading the headlines and deciding if I wanted to commit to the article. Unconsciously, I was searching to find anything on John Doe. Skip anything to do with the economy--too depressing. The headlines were fairly predictable: The local theater was opening a new show; a spotlight on a new business in town; and the high school sports highlights. Occasionally, I'd read about a bar scuffle accompanied by a few arrests. I checked the names, making sure Donny wasn't involved. I checked every corner of the paper, even the corners near Dear Abby and celebrity news, but found nothing about John Doe. I guess he was old news. But he woke up. Isn't that newsworthy?

A man entered the store at about 10 a.m. and started to peruse the cases. He was your typical North Idahoan--jeans and a flannel--nothing too fancy, but I could tell he was a quiet man with inner strength, the kind everyone respects, the kind who wears a big belt buckle and is weathered around the edges.

"Good morning. Can I help you find something?" I said in a gentle, welcoming voice. Dad had always told me to be cheery and soft. The first impression is the only impression you get in a jewelry store. Like a used-car lot, customers have the instinct to hide and skedaddle when approached with excessive enthusiasm.

He exhaled and spoke calloused, "I'm looking for something for my wife, and I'm not quite sure what will do."

A project. Thank goodness. A perfect distraction. "Is there a special occasion?"

He looked at me, as if he was angry. "I wouldn't call it special. My wife is sick."

"I'm sorry to hear that. Were you thinking a necklace, a ring, a bracelet?"

His voice suddenly became very quiet, "She's given her whole life to raising our boys. She's got a tough battle ahead." He wasn't talking to me, but getting it out. This purchase was more for him than for her.

"Would you like Lenora to design something for her, a token to represent your family?"

"I think so" was all he could say without risking his composure. He pulled a photo out of his billfold, tattered, as if it had been there for

81

years. He tossed it onto the glass counter, not able to look at me. It was a picture of four boys on a fishing trip. "This is her essence."

The boys were in camouflage and all looked like Dad. I took the photo in my hand, asking, "May I share this with Lenora? She can return it." He nodded.

I took down the names and birthdates of each family member, and told him that I'd call when Lenora completed the project. He seemed grateful, and actually cracked a gentle smile on his way out.

Being in the jewelry business brings in all sorts of clientele, from those in love to those in the doghouse. Occasionally, you meet the tragic stories. Dad told me that he never got used to the sad ones, but to remember that jewelry is a token, a symbol for expressing love, and hope.

I didn't know what I would make for her, but I knew it wouldn't be a ring. Fingers either swell or shrink when people are sick and on medication. I don't think a necklace or bracelet, because the skin often becomes extremely sensitive and frail. I sat, rubbing the edges of the worn photo, as if channeling the mother of these beautiful boys, my mind searching for the perfect gift of hope.

The front bell jingled softly and a cold draft swept in. Her back faced me as she shut the door, although the door would glide shut eventually. I hardly recognized her in street clothes. Mira looked different without her hospital scrubs. Her face was serious, almost nervous. Her dark black hair was draped over her sweater, unlike the tight ponytail she wore while nursing. My mind started racing, wondering why she was in our shop. Was Jack dead? Did something go horribly wrong?

"I'm sorry to intrude at work." Mira's face was stale, tired.

"Why are you here?" I was desperate to know.

"Look," Mira was fidgeting, looking around the room nervously, "I'm stepping way beyond my professional standards here. Mira tapped her fingers on her pants. "Jack is awake and asking for you. I know it may be scary, wondering if he's going to be different," she hesitated. "He's talking. Not much, but talking. He says your name, mostly."

I was still holding the photo of the boys, grabbing it as if I were holding on for balance. My voice was low, confessional, as I looked into the photo. "I don't expect you to understand my intentions, but by me staying away, I'm doing the right thing. I should have never come in the first place."

I looked up to see that Mira was facing me with an incredulous stare, yet her eyes were focused elsewhere--beyond me--into a distant memory.

"Have you ever been rejected?" she asked, her eyes now blazing into mine. She wasn't nervous; she was fiery.

"No." I answered truthfully.

"Rejection is ultimate pain. It fills you with doubt, fear, isolation, hopelessness--all at once." Mira looked vulnerable yet angry. "I learned a lot from you and Jack, or I thought I did. You have no idea how watching you with Jack has changed me."

"Changed you?" Now I was confused.

"I have been chasing," Mira laughs in recollection, "the wrong man . . . a married man, like a desperate, sick, washed-up old nurse." She smiled at me, admitting her self-loathing. "I've dabbled in online dating, with total failure. Nothing really works out for me. But because of you--hearing your story--I've realized that I need to be someone worth chasing. No one ever told me that before." Mira was confiding in me, like a little girl who needed to be loved. "Watching you love him . . . There's just something about him, and you. I've been so alive, giving my best to my job, for you and for Jack . . . and for me."

"You misunderstood," was all I could say. I felt like a needle, about to pop her Macy's Day Parade balloon.

"What is there to misunderstand?" she was clenching her teeth, nearly hysterical.

My body was shaking, and I couldn't control it. I could feel the hot blood flowing to my eyes, my nose. *Don't cry,* I tried to convince myself. It was a nervous reaction that was unstoppable. If I attempted to speak, the tears would flow, and I would be a pathetic, blubbering mess. I stood statuesque, refusing to lose composure, waiting for my pulse to slow down so that I could tell her the truth.

Mira broke the silence. "I know you're young. I also know that you don't quit on people when they are sick. At least *good* people don't."

We stared at each other momentarily, until Mira turned out the door. Her words stung. Mira's accusations were misguided, I knew, but some hint of truth rang in them. I was quitting on Jack.

Being there for him now would be more complicated. He was conscious. It didn't take long for me to conclude that seeing Jack one last time was the right thing to do, to give him closure, and to tell the truth. One last dinner with him, and then I would say goodbye and face the consequences.

I was now squeezing the picture of the four boys in my hand. I tried my best to straighten it back out and taped it to a piece of cardstock. I pinned it to the wall in the studio. The boys were strong, you could tell, and close, the way you hope all brothers are.

Donny came barging into the shop, edgy in his usual way. "When are your parents coming home?"

I knew what he wanted. About halfway through every month, Donny ran out of cash. Between Dad and Dawn, he was able to scrape enough sympathy to recover what he had overindulged on the first half of the month. It annoyed me that both adults in his life didn't stand up to him. They both caved when he pleaded for a hand-out.

"Two-and-a-half weeks. Call Dawn. She always feels sorry for you."

Donny was behind the counter, rummaging through the office, looking for petty cash.

"Do you mind? This is not a u-serve cash cow." I was annoyed that he thought he could just plow through the office.

"I'm sorry if I don't have everything at my fingertips, like some people I know." That was the usual jab that Donny gave, and its effect was nil.

"Donny, why do you make everything so difficult?" I really wanted to know.

"I guess some of us just don't live in Never-Never land."

"I am not willing to grow up? That's funny, Donny, coming from you."

"You work with Daddy, you live in Daddy's loft, and you do everything to be perfect in his eyes.

But the problem is you have no life. You have this perfect little existence all wrapped up in ribbons and bows . . . Margaret Whitaker, prodigy jewelry maker, a.k.a. Lenora. Well, some of us have to bus tables and scrape gravy off plates to make a buck. Does that make me less than you? I guess it does when the economy goes south and nobody's tipping right now. So sorry if I need a handout! I wouldn't want *you* to stoop so low."

"You scrape gravy off plates?" I wondered what happened to the Ski & Skate Shop job. But it was apparent to me that he probably lost that job too. "Look, I have *never* criticized your job, Donny. I just question your choices."

"My choices? What choices do I have?"

I didn't want to continue. I could never win an argument with Donny. I was not going to point out his illegal activity that was the obvious drain on his funds, because he knew how to make me look stupid. He always did.

"There's nothing here. Sorry. Try the bank." End of discussion.

"I don't know what Wyn sees in you," he muttered, and then headed out the door, slamming it with a bang.

This unpleasant encounter with my cousin stole all creative energy from me, and I spent the rest of the afternoon doodling designs for the sick woman and nothing seemed right. I had a booklet full of crossed-out pencil scratches.

I couldn't concentrate, for fear of what I knew I must do tonight. Nobody had stepped foot in Whitaker Jewelry for the last three hours, and it was half an hour till closing. I locked up the shop early to take a little extra time to spruce up before going to the hospital.

In my loft, I tried on at least three different outfits. Dress pants seemed too formal. Khaki pants seemed homely. I settled on my favorite jeans, the knees faded out. *Did they make me look too young? What does it matter? This is a one and done visit.* I settled on a terracotta sweater, complemented with a simple 14-karat-gold teardrop necklace with an amber stone. I didn't want to seem too desperate.

I spent extra time in the bathroom, applying the makeup that I forgot I even owned. I fussed with the blush so that it was perfectly natural, and reapplied the golden-hued eye shadow three times so that it complemented my shirt without overpowering it. I toyed with my hair, wondering if my auburn locks were too wild, and if I should flatiron them. I tried pulling it back but thought letting it fall naturally would show a more mature look. Just a spritz of perfume, a dab of lipstick, and there appeared a woman in the mirror that I hardly recognized.

I grabbed my keys and jacket, when the doorbell rang. I skipped down the stairs to check whom it could be. Through the peephole I saw Wyn with his hands behind his back. I opened the door slowly.

Wyn's eyes popped. "You look--wow."

I smiled at him, although my nerves were thick. "I'm on my way out."

"Oh." He looked disappointed. "You got a date or something?" He quickly realized he hit the nail on the head when I didn't respond. "Oh, the old guy." Wyn said.

"Did you need something?" I asked, as if nothing was awkward.

Wyn revealed a package wrapped in brown paper. "I brought you a piece of glass, for the frame I broke." He handed me the brown package. "I had it cut to fit, for the one of you and your Dad skiing."

"My favorite picture. Thank you."

"You're welcome." Wyn turned away, walking toward his truck. "See you in the morning, Maggie."

****

Kootenai Medical Center was the same, sterile place. I pulled my visitor's badge from my purse and flashed it at the receptionist, who then buzzed me in the double doors. I walked to the Neuro unit, the familiar pathway I had been so many times, and looked for Mira at her station. She was not there. Instead, it was an older nurse, maybe late fifties, with thick, short black hair and a round face.

As I approached the nurses' station, Dr. James came pacing around the corner. He was making rounds, nearly skidding to a halt when he saw me. "Margaret?"

I felt meek, immature in his presence. "Dr. James," was all I could think to say.

Resting his hand on my shoulder, I noticed his golden wedding ring. He pulled me off to an uninhabited wall, whispering gently, "You okay?" When I didn't respond, he continued, "This is tough stuff, I know. I want you to know that Jack is showing signs that his mind is intact. Every day he improves. He's really, really lucky."

What did this mean? How much did Jack know? How was I going to go through with this?

"Let's walk in. He's been asking for you." Dr. James put his hand on my back to prod me forward and continued talking in a hushed voice. "You'll notice that his speech is somewhat slurred. That's normal and should improve with speech therapy." He smiled at me and continued, "Also, sometimes patients are hyperemotional. It's part of the brain's readjustment to motor sensory--"

"Wait!" This was happening too fast. I hadn't lined things up right yet. "Dr. James, I need to ask you something, you and your staff."

"Sure, Margaret, what is it?"

"Can you please give me the space . . . give us the freedom to take a step back in our relationship. No engagement, fiancé, wedding talk?"

He saw the pain in my eyes, the confusion, and I could tell he knew this pain before. "Of course. I'll let the staff know."

Which brought me to my next question: "Where's Mira? I need to talk to Mira."

"Mira requested a schedule change. She works the morning shift now." There was an uncharacteristic lack of concern in his voice, as he spoke cold and terse.

Sensing the awkwardness, Dr. James smiled warmly again, took my elbow and walked me slowly into room 331, stopping just inches outside the curtain. I heard Dr. James explain, "Jack, there's someone here to see you." Dr. James came back around the curtain and pulled me in. My heart was racing, about to explode. There he was, sitting up while resting his head on his pillow, his eyes still closed.

"He is still on some pretty strong sedatives, so he's going to be drowsy." Dr. James pulled a chair next to the bed for me. He leaned over Jack, putting his hand on his shoulder. "Jack. You have a visitor."

Jade. That was the color of his eyes, as he rolled them open, not focusing on one specific place--dark eyelashes and jade eyes.

"Margaret is here to see you." Dr. James was leaning in to his face, speaking loudly.

"Maya?" he whispered, looking at the doctor.

"Mar-gar-et," Dr. James enunciated. He turned to me and told me, "With the jaw bone broken, he will slur his words. We're lucky he can talk. Don't be too alarmed when things come out funny."

Jack turned to me and stared right into me. His face was dull, expressionless. I stared right back into his dark stubbly face. They say the eyes are the window to the soul. We were both entranced, reading each other through that window. His eyes suddenly rolled away.

Jack took two big breaths, as if speaking took all his energy. "I don't re--re-mber." He looked down at his bed sheets, lost in frustration.

Cruel. That was the only word that came to my mind. I know so much more about him than he knows about himself. I can't burden him with explaining the lie. I muttered the words, "I'll come back later," as I turned to walk out.

Dr. James grabbed my arm, whispering in my ear, "No. You have to stay. I know it's hard, but he *will* remember. He is showing every sign of full recovery. He needs you."

"I don't think I can--"

"You can. And you will. Help him remember. Talk to him." He had no idea that this wouldn't work. He pointed to the red call button, "If you need help." Dr. James squeezed my arm in encouragement, tightening his lips together, a sort of rally for my courage. He paced out of the room.

I turned around and Jack was staring. His eyes were sad, lost. I sat down next to him, this time without the freedom to touch him, caress him. I sat on my hands.

"Are you okay?" *Dumb question, Mags.* What else am I to say?

"I don-know." His speech was slurred, but his mind *was* there. He looked at me with those frustrated, apologetic jade-green eyes. "Who are you?"

I smiled at him. He was already better at making conversation than I was. "I'm Margaret. Margaret Whitaker."

"Ma--" he stumbled, as if trying to recall. The words weren't forming. Frustration settled in. "Ma-ya."

"M. You can call me just E-m." Margaret was a lot to spit out, and nobody claimed that nickname on me yet. "I've been here with you in the hospital. You've been all alone." I reached out for his hand and put mine on top. He looked up at me, almost recognizing my touch.

"Alone?" He looked confused. "Where--May-a?"

"Maya? There's no Maya. Mira is the nurse. She spends a lot of time with you. And I'm Margaret, or M for short. No Maya, just me." I sat and looked at him, his frustrated expression still exposing his confusion.

"Than-kyou" he strained, relaxing his shoulders into the pillow again.

"You're welcome." This was going better than I thought. Now I just needed to wrap it up, say my goodbyes, and he was going to be okay. I could tell.

"You do know what happened to you?" This was the perfect segue to explain that he was alone, and I volunteered to sit with him.

He nodded. "Acc-dent. I don't re-mber."

"Do you know who you are, your name?"

He took a long time and then whispered, "Peter."

Peter. Well, I wonder if this had come up yet. I personally liked Jack, but Peter suited him, especially with the beard.

"Peter, I am just a guest, a volunteer, someone who was here to help you fight the big fight. And you made it. You're going to be okay. There are a lot of really amazing staff here at the hospital, and they're going to get you back on your feet in no time."

Peter's eyes widened in recollection, "My face," he muttered. "My face . . . shave cream."

"You want to shave?" Maybe he was a little childish; of all the things to worry about.

"I was going--shave." Jack, or now Peter, placed one hand gently on his face.

"I can let the nurse know, and I'm sure she can get you some supplies."

Peter was closing his eyes, distressed, and stroking his face. Something was really bothering him about his thick stubble.

I could feel my inward pull of helping hurt animals, the draw to be a nurturer tempting me to stay with him, although it was the perfect time to leave. "Peter, would you like to shave?"

He looked up at me and then sadly down at my hand on top of his remaining hand, tears coming again. "M, I love you."

Hyperemotional. I had been warned of this. I took initiative and stood up. "I'll go find a razor," and I walked out of the room and found the new nurse at the station.

"He wants to shave," I whispered nervously to her.

Without a word, she put down paperwork that she was involved in, stood up quickly and confidently from behind the station, and walked around me. I followed her into Jack's room, where she opened up a cabinet near the sink and gathered a plastic basin and towel. She nearly slapped them into my stomach, a woman on a mission. "I'll be right in with a razor and cream." That was it. I guess this was normal. Men need to shave.

Filling the tub with warm water, I prepared to shave this stranger. Peter's eyes were closed again, the drugs taking their sedative effect. I placed the towel on a moving stand, rolled it next to him, and gently set the water basin on top, only an inch full. His eyes reopened.

"Now, you're going to have to help me here. This is my first time." Peter's eyes warmed, looking beyond me, an attempt at a smile seeped in the corner of his mouth. "Hi," he whispered beyond me.

A voice from behind caught me off guard. "Look at you, handsome," Mira said. She didn't make eye contact with me, but put her hand on his shoulder, speaking directly to him. "Decided to clean up a little, Jack?" She handed me a razor and a travel size can of shave cream.

"Jack?" he questioned, until I interrupted.

"Peter. He likes to be called Peter now." I hoped she wouldn't overthink this. "It's a first-name, middle-name thing."

"Record Keeping is going to flip with all the paperwork corrections," Mira moaned.

I didn't want her to see my guilt showing, so I sprayed shaving cream into my palm. I had seen men shaving on commercials as well as my dad a few times, and that was all I had to go by. Dad had one of those electric razors, and he just buzzed it all around his stubble; he was no where near as hairy as Peter. I spread the shaving cream on his beard, down his jaw, and onto his neck. The razor had a safety seal. I opened it, to find a double-edged blade. Was I supposed to go against the hair, or with it? It didn't really matter. I could only shave about one inch until I had to rinse. His stubble was thick, so it was a lot to take off. This was going to take a while.

"I'll get another razor," Mira spoke aloud, and left the room. I had forgotten she was there.

Peter was looking at me, trying to keep his eyes steady. "Maya."

"Just M."

"M, who are you?" he asked again.

Mira entered from behind, "Your fiancé, you lucky dog. You're getting married."

Peter sat there, shaving cream on his face, confused. "Just don't think about it right now," I said to Peter, to clear his confusion. I shot Mira a look that made it clear that I wasn't happy with her interjection. I didn't even hear her come in, and her black Dansko shoes were silent. When did nurses start wearing black rubber-soled shoes? "Close your eyes, rest." I placed my hands over his eyes to induce his relaxation. I also took a moment to close my own eyes and take a deep breath.

Mira took her razor and shaved Peter's beard. I sat, with the razor resting in my palm, looking at the floor, tears streaming down my eyes. *What a mess. What a mess I've made.*

"Stop with the self-pity already," Mira accused. "We can do this together." We shaved Peter's face, one on each side, the tub floating with black hair and cream. His chest began to rise and fall with each deep inhale and exhale he took. He was asleep, again.

Mira began to talk in a low, matronly voice. "I'm glad you came, Margaret. I know I was a bit harsh the other day, but I've grown kind of fond of this one. He's sweet. He deserves to have someone—"

"I know." My annoyance with her presence began to show. "Don't mention our engagement or call me his fiancé. Obviously, we're not going through with it."

"I see." She was finishing the last strokes, making a clean sweep across his entire face with the razor. I took a washcloth and wiped his silky-smooth face clean.

"Thanks," I said.

"It's what I do, clean people up." Mira sat back and stared at Peter, uncomfortably long. She then slowly turned to look at me. My pulse raced, wondering what was conspiring in her mind. Suddenly, she stood up. "I'm off. Just came to get my paycheck."

I only then realized Mira was not in scrubs but in jeans and a tee shirt. There was unease in the way she spoke to me. Maybe her cynical nature was creeping back.

"Dr. James told me you changed shifts?" I was testing my private inklings, at the very moment Dr. James walked into the room.

Mira instantly looked to the floor. "See you around, Margaret." She began to walk out of the room, without acknowledging Dr. James.

After a moment of uncomfortable silence, Dr. James smiled at me and then at sleeping Peter. "Well, who do we have here?" Dr. James examined Peter's cleaned-up visage.

"Peter, he wants to be called Peter now-- middle-name thing. He kept asking for a shave. Mira helped me out, thank God." Dr. James bit his lip, smiling.

"You know, when a patient regains consciousness, things are very basal for awhile. Patients can be very childlike . . . simple. It's very sweet at times, the things they ask for. It can be trying too."

"I've noticed."

"Every time you come, something good happens for this fellow. Don't be a stranger anymore, okay?" It was more of an expectation than a request. "Tomorrow I'm scheduling his first physical therapy appointment. The sooner we get him back to basic activities, the quicker the brain re-registers. I'd like you to be there."

"Me?" I was just about to say goodbye to Peter and leave on good terms.

"He needs support now more than ever. Relearning basic skills can be overwhelmingly frustrating."

"My job--"

Dr. James interrupted, "I'll write a medical note, if necessary. Your boss would have to accept that." I refrained from admitting that I was the boss and sole employee of Whitaker Jewelry, currently. "I've scheduled for 10 a.m., right after breakfast, after a good night's rest. We'll start the first session right here, and then we'll discuss transferring him to a rehabilitation center." At that, Dr. James vanished out the door.

Great, I was committed to one more day with him. Peter. I had to remember the name change.

"Peter?" He was asleep. I put my hand on his calloused, yet freshly-shaven, soft face. Nothing about him was young or juvenile, yet I found him lovely. Life had planted its imprint on Peter. "Sleep well."

As I neared the door to leave, I heard him mutter, choking. "Ma-ya. Ma--"

As I turned, the disheveled stranger I named Jack was no more. He was now Peter, the beautiful jade-eyed man whom I helped fight the fight. His eyes were open, studying me.

"M. Just M for now," I whispered.

"Do you . . . love . . . me?" He pleaded, distress coming through his voice.

I looked at him, through the window of his soul, and saw a frightened man, begging for truth. "Of course I do." For the first time, our eyes locked, an infinitesimal second of truth between us. The play was becoming the thing.

He relaxed, closing his eyes to sleep again. I turned and left the room, disorientation and elation overtaking me.

Chapter Seven: Home

Mother Theresa once said that the most basic need in all of humanity is not clothing, food, nor shelter: it is the need to be wanted. * I had always felt wanted, by my parents. I knew I was blessed with a family that was unlike so many, with a mother and father who truly loved each other at sixty-seven years old. I guess I wanted to be wanted, not by my parents, but by another individual--to be desired as the object of someone's utter affection.

Peter wanted me. Sure, he was on medication, but there was a loveable man who wanted me. I had never felt more confident about my cause to help him since the day at Chinese Gardens when I was called to him.

Every morning I went to his physical therapy appointments, and every night I went and had dinner with him. I was able to close the store according to my schedule, and reopen it when I was available. Business was still painfully slow.

Day after day, Peter improved, in speech, in movement and, slowly, in memory. Peter remembered odd things about his life, like that he dislikes olives and does not own or believe in cell phones. Cell phones are an interruption on human connection, he argued. He proved this several times as my cell phone rang, once when Julie

called and a couple times when Wyn called. I
learned to turn off the phone when I was with him.

Peter did not remember where he lived and
especially did not remember living with me, which
he apologized for continually. The hardest part for
him was that he didn't remember me at all and
only remembered a front door with a D on it.

The deeper I got involved with his therapy, the
easier it was to continue the lie. I was able to push
that little inconvenience away, believing that I was
Margaret Whitaker, personal assistant to Peter the
miracle man. The line between reality and fiction
wasn't just starting to blur. It was a watercolor
bleeding down the canvas, ending in a puddle of
brown. I loved being with him, and wanted to
protect the lie for as long as I could. I was now
Peter's girl. It gave me purpose and him hope.

The two weeks after he woke up were pure
adrenaline. The endorphin high that I was missing
every morning on my canceled runs with Wyn were
easily replaced with a surge of dopamine and
oxytocin, the adrenaline and love drugs,
administered by my brain after every visit with
Peter. I would come home after our dinner visit
and feverishly create in the studio. Sleep was
pointless; I was wired. Like a writer with an
effective muse, my artistic inspiration was
sprinting through my veins. In my normal life, if I
was busy, I would create in the back studio while
Dad ran the front office. My normal life was gone--
Dad was still on the last leg of his cruise, and I
had some projects to fill. Nighttime was truly my
only option.

With all the love in my heart, I poured out the
emotions into my designs. The man with the sick
wife came in to preview the broach I had designed

for him, and he loved it. I made a solid gold tree, representing the life she had given her sons, and now the life she was fighting for. On the tree were four jewels, the fruit in their birthstones. Encircling the tree were two eternity bands, looping through each other. Everything was intertwined, yet independent. I caught the man wiping a tear from his eye after he paid for his purchase.

The only little kink in my new situation was Wyn. I canceled my morning run with Wyn after seeing Peter awake in the hospital. I'm sure he had a good idea why, but I really didn't care what Wyn thought. The next day I texted again, to let him know it would be more of a temporary hiatus. Wyn didn't respond.

Late one night, as I was elbow deep in wax mold and firing up molten metals ready to be poured, I heard a knock on the front door. It wasn't convenient to answer the door, nor was it safe. I had no choice but to ignore the knocks. Suddenly, I heard the door bustle open, chattering noise and lots of commotion. I froze, slowly turning off my torch. I set the metal mold holder down into the metal bowl, causing a clang. I reached for the phone, nearly dialing 911 when Donny's voice called out, "M.C.? You back there?"

I slammed the phone down, praying it didn't connect. "Geez, Donny. I about called the cops!" Donny knew how to break into any place, and knew the wiring on this building especially. I turned the corner to see Donny with Wyn, Victor and Red. "Have you ever thought of calling?"

"Your phone's not on," Wyn said. "We were out and thought you might want to join us for midnight bowling."

100

"You broke into the shop, for midnight bowling? Unbelievable, Donny."

"I'll reset everything on the way out. The light was on. You could have been bound and gagged and . . . I'm supposed to be looking out for you, you know."

"Says who?" I had a feeling I knew. As much as Dad always said he trusted me, that I was the most trustworthy of kids he's ever known, there was a real protective quality about him that he couldn't hide. Donny was the one who needed protecting, but nobody asked me to look out for him. "Don't answer that. I already know."

"I take it you're not interested?" Donny said.

Even if I could use some time away, I couldn't let this creative vein escape me. The city was putting on an Art Walk on Friday night, and I was hoping to recoup some lost business.

"I've got to finish pouring some molds. The metal's already solidifying, and I've got to work with it, quick."

Donny didn't care. He was thumbing through Dad's old collection of CDs. "All right, Mags. Just offering you a chance to get out and have a little fun." Donny went from moseying through Dad's shelves, to noticing a few pieces I had cast, work that I had poured in the last few nights of inspiration. "You've been busy." That was about as good of a compliment as I would ever get out of him.

I fired up the blowtorch and started to heat the silver back up. "Don't forget to lock up." Donny and the boys left. I put my safety goggles on and started to reheat the metal. There was a figure still in the doorway. Wyn. I didn't have time for Wyn right now.

He approached, reading my body language, yet still pursuing a conversation. He commented on my rows of new pieces that I had recently poured, a few rings, mostly broaches and necklace pendants. "You did these?"

"It's what I do." I was cold, but I was using a blowtorch, and talking wasn't ideal at the moment.

"They're nice," he said.

"You know, this is kind of a science, and if I overheat this silver, it's going to melt the mold and won't set properly."

"Just tell me one thing." Wyn was ignoring my request. "Promise me that if you ever get into trouble, you'll call."

"I'm not ten," I said sarcastically.

"I know. It's just, you won't tell anyone what you're doing--where you go, and with whom."

"That's the privilege of being an adult, Wyn." I snapped, and then instantly felt bad. I turned off the blowtorch; the silver would have to wait. "Not that this is your business, but you'd find out sooner or later. His name's Peter. I met him in the hospital. He's got no one. I've been there for him, and we've grown close. End of story."

Wyn looked shell-shocked. "The John Doe?"

"Yes, the John Doe. Don't worry about me. I'm the one who's fine. He's not."

Wyn looked disappointed, apologetic. "I shouldn't have assumed."

"Yeah, that's never a good idea." I flared up the blowtorch again. "If you don't mind," I started to heat the metal, "I might be able to salvage this piece."

Suddenly music sounded through the speakers. A loud thumping grew from subtle to booming, the base turned up full throttle. Wyn and

102

I both froze, as if on Candid Camera. The piercing cry of the Little River Band's infamous song, "Lonesome Loser" blasted through the surround sound speakers.

"You're an ass!" Wyn yelled toward the front shop, where Donny was waiting along with Victor and Red.

"Let's go, loser!" Donny shouted back. Wyn's throat turned red, as he shook his head and couldn't even muster a goodbye. Instead, I'm fairly sure I heard a dogpile when Wyn met up with Donny in the front room. After a small commotion, the front door jingled and they left. I could finally giggle, while enjoying the rest of the song with my blowtorch.

I worked all night long, pouring metal into the pre-etched wax molds that I had laid out--just me, the music, and the studio. I created all night, until the sun rose over the lake and illuminated cold, frosty Tubbs Hill behind our building. The quiet allowed me to think, rationalize and craft the confession that I needed to give Peter. He was improving--remembering things--and soon he would realize that I'm not Maya, whom he kept calling for. The time was here. The truth must be told.

It was seven o'clock in the morning and the all-nighter was starting to have its effect on me. I knew that I was momentarily manic. I couldn't sleep, so I didn't even try.

I closed the shop and returned to my loft to take a quick shower and freshen up. After debating what the perfect breakup outfit should be, I settled on jeans and a black scoop neck sweater. I assembled a purse and threw in a camera just in case things went well.

I entered the hospital through my usual route, recognizing and knowing the names of nearly every employee. The receptionist welcomed me warmly, waving me her usual good-morning salute. I bit my lip and smiled back.

Mira wasn't at the station, as usual. In fact, the halls were eerily silent, the fluorescent yellow lights glowing on the glossy-waxed cement floors. I walked into room 331, but Peter was not there. His bed gown was folded neatly on the unmade bed. Next to the bed, there was a folder filled with pamphlets, checklists, and a book on TBI: Traumatic Brain Injuries and Recovery.

A small commotion was heard down the hall. I heard Mira laughing. I walked out of the room to find Mira supporting Peter around the waist. Dr. James, as well as the physical therapist, walked beside him.

"M!" was the first word out of his mouth. "Look at me!" The staff was tickled pink, everyone's hard work coming to fruition, sprinkled with a dose of good luck.

I was confused by the rally of emotion--slightly jealous that I was left out of the excitement, yet I felt overwhelmingly relieved that he was walking again. This unexpected joy masked the dread I was hiding of what I was about to confess.

"Peter is walking, independently." Mira took her arm off his waist and let him go.

Peter wasn't swaggering, as if he could tip over, like he had done for the past two weeks in physical therapy. He was solid. "The sea legs are gone. I'm back!" He walked right to me, put his big arms around me, and kissed me right there in front of the staff.

I could hear clapping from Dr. James and the physical therapist. My head was spinning. This wasn't part of the plan. Hyperemotional, that was all.

Mira came to our side and took Peter by the waist. "Easy there. We don't want you lightheaded. We've got a lot to go over if you are going to be discharged tomorrow." She walked him to room 331, while I waited for Dr. James. The physical therapist joined them in room 331, while I spoke to the doctor outside.

"He's passed all twelve of the physical requirements for us to release him. He's ready." The smile on Dr. James' face was tender.

"When?" I asked.

"Tomorrow morning. I know it seems sudden, but with medical costs, we can't keep him longer if he's improving so quickly. He doesn't even qualify for in-house rehabilitation. It's really a miracle."

"You can't send him home. What if he regresses?" Panic was setting in.

"He'll need physical therapy three times a week. But he can live at home. He doesn't qualify for inpatient care." Dr. James knew as well as I did that I'm the one who's not ready. "We can arrange a home nurse for two weeks."

"No. No-o." I was not going to bring any more of this into my life.

"Okay, then I'll just need to go over some things that you'll need to have ready by tomorrow. I've got a checklist of supplies you'll need, some to be sent with you, and some that you'll need to pick up. In addition, I'll have the first week of medications sent up by the pharmacy, and then I'll give you a prescription for the next three months."

I was starting to feel dizzy. *Don't lose it. Breathe. You always figure things out. Just keep breathing.* "I need to speak with Peter, before he comes home. If you'll excuse me," I tried to escape the lecture from Dr. James, but it wasn't so easy.

"I've got a huge workload today, and the checkout procedure is quite lengthy, so I was hoping to get started. I'll make this as brief as possible." Dr. James reached behind the nurses' station and presented a manila folder filled with documents. "If you can start signing waivers and releases, then he can get out of here faster. Paperwork drives this place, unfortunately." He began with a stack of papers as thick as the Sunday newspaper.

I signed document after document, acknowledging the risks, liabilities, procedures for proper care, and expectations and suggestions. I acknowledged that the hospital staff explained everything to me, and that I had no further questions. After about an hour, Dr. James said, "Relationships aren't easy. Marriage isn't easy. Feelings come and go. The commitment's the glue—solid commitment, no matter what. Some people discover it earlier than others, but it always catches up with you. You either commit or you don't." It must have been a pep talk that he gives often to wide-eyed spouses after signing their free life away. It felt like a reprimand, or maybe a warning.

Peter was finishing the last of his speech therapy in room 331. He was sitting in the chair next to his bed, Mira tidying up the room, while he repeated words. "Evening, everyone, evening, everyone . . ." I walked in quietly, not wanting to interrupt, but Peter straightened up, exclaiming, "Hey, Mar–gar–et . . . Margaret!"

I smiled back at him. He had a beautiful smile and looked handsome in street clothes. I wondered how he would look when he's angry.

The physical therapist collected his chart and mentioned, "Dr. James did give you the schedule for physical therapy appointments?" I nodded. "Then we'll see you soon." He winked, and then put his hand on Peter's shoulder, "I'll be seeing you three times a week, Peter. Your success depends on your dedication to practicing at home."

Peter looked at me. "Home." He stood up, walked to me, and wrapped his arms around me. "I'm coming home." I wondered when the hyperemotional thing would wear off. His embrace went on, and on, and he held on for dear life. When he let go, he exclaimed, "You're very cute!" This made me laugh. I was pitiful.

Mira stood up to leave, offering us some privacy. "Would you mind taking our picture?" I asked. I dug my camera out of my purse.

Mira took the camera and stood stiffly in front of us. "Well, act like you like each other at least." Peter put his arm around me and smiled. I melted into him, fighting the tear I could feel forming. She snapped a photo and quickly handed me the camera, before turning to leave.

I followed her to the room door, closing it gently so I could have a private moment with Peter. My mind was racing with how I should adjust my confession. There was no way he could come home with me. I lived in a loft, twenty steps above a jewelry shop. I was not his girlfriend or his fiancé. I was a volunteer. This facade had to stop, now.

I sat on the freshly made, crisp hospital bed. Peter sat next to me. The nervous tension between us was palpable. I suddenly felt like a little girl with her father. I wish I could just come out and confess: I stole the candy in the candy jar. It was me. But there was more at stake than a slapped hand.

"Jack, I need to tell you something." I was so nervous I could hardly speak.

"Jack?" he looked puzzled.

"What? Peter."

"No, you said *Jack*." He looked puzzled, calculating.

Ignoring the faux pas, "Peter, I'm scared. I don't know if I can bring you home."

"I'm scared too. I'm not remembering things. Maybe if I get home, I'll remember more . . . of us."

"Well, that's the thing. There can't be an 'us.' I mean, if you can't remember us, then our history is gone, like it was never there. And that's just not any way I want to start--continue a relationship. Does that make any sense?"

"The only thing that makes sense is that you come here, everyday." Here it was again, the call to help, to comfort, to support, and now to commit.

"Peter, I am not sure I can do this anymore." He put his large hands on my temples and kissed me, out of the blue again, a big, long, emotional kiss. My stomach surged with pins and needles.

Still holding my head in his hands, he urged, "I'll remember. Don't give up on me." And he kissed me again, punctuating his request.

I have never been a liar. I have prided myself with living a life of integrity. However, I have learned that you can rationalize nearly anything to justify a greater means. Like in Les Miserables,

108

Jean Valjean steals bread to keep his family from starving. Yes, the crime was punishable for five years' imprisonment, and the numerous attempts to escape the torturous labor prison earned him fourteen more, but survival should not be a crime.

****

Donny needed money, and I needed to get ready for Peter's homecoming. I paid Donny one hundred bucks to buy some of his items, like his green bedsheets and brown throw blanket. I told him that I wouldn't ask him what he needed the money for, if he wouldn't ask me what I need the bedsheets for. He agreed. I also inquired if he could spare an outfit or two. I'm pretty sure he knew I was helping out the John Doe, and in the spirit of charity, Donny was surprisingly helpful.

I worked all night, forgoing my usual studio time, and used my nervous energy to redecorate the loft. I replaced the picture of Dad and me skiing with the picture of Peter and me in the hospital. I stripped everything from the loft that looked feminine and juvenile, from the polka-dotted bedsheets to the purple shower curtain, and changed them out for dark green and browns. Mom had a few watercolor paintings that I couldn't part with, but the plants from the shop that I borrowed and Donny's brown throw gave the place a masculine feel. I could imagine Peter resting here, recovering after his long, sterile hospital stay.

I had planned an all-out guttural confession at the hospital yesterday, which never materialized. Now, it was appearing that I should not confess so abruptly. It was still my intention to fully confess to Peter, in time. For Peter's sake, I would take it slower, to help him transition. I would chip away at the truth, so as not to send him into shock. If he got to know me, he would know that I meant well, and still do.

However, the three kisses we had shared consumed my every thought. I relived them in my mind constantly. The first when he was walking in the hospital. The second two, when I shared with him that our relationship couldn't continue as it had before. I was bonded to him. I loved him. I loved him fighting for his life. I loved that he appreciated me, regardless that he couldn't remember me. He could feel the love I held for him, and he returned it with every smile, and with those kisses.

The morning of his release, I had figured there would be a spectacle, a potential mishap, or even a total recognition of my fraud. But Dr. James wasn't on site, nor was the neurosurgeon or physical therapist. Just Mira, who told me all farewells were given the evening prior. Mira, in her final goodbye, told him that he was her miracle patient, and that his courage changed her. She hugged him for a long time, and although she tried to hide it, I noticed her wiping her eyes.

I drove the short two miles to Sherman Avenue slowly, as if a newborn baby was in the car and I was terrified to jostle its unsteady head. In silence, Peter took in the orange, brown and red colors of Coeur d'Alene. When I pulled up to the back alley, Peter sat still in the car. "We're here," I informed him.

Peter lacked any recognition, and I knew it. There was an overpowering sadness, a gray hovering in the air.

I couldn't do it. I couldn't take the lie into the loft, above the shop, into my home. "Peter," I began, but the burning in my throat prevented me from continuing.

"M," he turned and stared into my scared eyes, "where am I?"

My leg started twitching, as if I were drumming a very fast beat on the drums. I couldn't look at him. I stared at the steering wheel, hoping the right words would reveal themselves. "I can't bring you home without you knowing the truth," I said.

Peter dropped his stare and looked straight out the window, suspicious of my sudden unease. I continued, "We are not, you and I..." I slowly pulled my eyes up to his and saw the puzzlement on his face, "I can't bring you into my home." I clenched my eyes shut, hoping that I wouldn't have to say anymore.

"I don't know this car. I don't know this driveway. I don't know this place." He looked at me for the first time with distrust.

"I tried to tell you," I whispered. "I tried to tell you," I repeated. "I tried to tell Mira. I tried to tell everybody. Nobody would listen to me."

"I'm listening." Peter demanded.

I sat. Silence screamed at me. My heartbeat was overpowering my mind. I took a deep breath to calm the noise in my body. "I read about you, John Doe. I read about you everyday in the paper-- all alone, fighting for your life. Nobody should be alone." I looked at him, and he was staring at me, stone cold. "I just meant to visit one time. And you started to improve. Everyone said it was because I finally showed up. Trust me when I say I tried to tell Mira and Dr. James, but nobody would listen." I was shaking.

"Who are you?" Peter repeated, this time enunciating each word. I was scared.

"Margaret Whitaker."

"How old are you, Margaret?" He was now interrogating me.

"Nineteen."

Peter's eyes froze and then tightened, as if he wanted to curse me out with all his might. His angry silence was worse. I heard a frantic noise, only to realize it was the nasal commotion of my own hyperventilation. After an eternity of painful silence, he exhaled firmly. "Nineteen." The sound of it sickened him, I could tell, and made me oddly aware of my juvenility. I had anticipated that he was older, maybe mid-twenties, but when he said thirty-two, even my gut wrenched.

"I only meant to help." That was my final grasp at justification.

Peter got out of the car, and slammed the door shut.

I got out slowly, watching him walk toward the lake. "Where are you going? You can't just leave. You don't even know who you are!" I knew it was a silly threat, and it was obvious he didn't know where he was going. It was cold, he had no money, no ID, no clue as to where he lived or who he really was.

Peter turned toward me, and then calmly walked back to me, stopping uncomfortably close to my face. The humiliation of my deception dissipated and was instantly replaced with primal fear. I felt terrified, not only as to what he was going to say, but what he may do. I was vulnerable, absolutely unprotected in the back alley behind Sherman Avenue. "You have no idea what you have done. You have no idea who I am."

I was a peon in the great game of life, an insignificant body that could be disposed of without a trace. I was playing with fire, had always been playing with fire, and never thought I could get burned. And yet, in the moment of my most dreaded fear--of revealing the lie--I was not focused on my survival, but his. "Please, just let me help you find home."

Peter stared with hatred in his eyes, until he turned his back on me and walked away. As he faded out of view, my entire body went numb-- incapable of moving, feeling, or reacting. I don't know how long I stood there, but I stood, in a trance, feeling the lie slowly ooze out of my body and free me. It was over. This made-up world of John Doe was over. I was free. I was lost.

Chapter Eight: Art Walk

I poured all my remaining energy, limited as it was, into Designs by Lenora. The fall Art Walk was in two days, and Whitaker Jewelry always participated in this monthly downtown event. During the days, I sat in a fog behind the counter, numb to the lack of business that was presenting itself slow as molasses. I couldn't read. I couldn't think. I couldn't do anything. I tried to focus as Lenora, with minor success, by etching wax molds of bangles, pendants, hair pins, cuff links-- anything but rings. I couldn't grasp the inspiration for love. During the evenings, I cast silver and gold, the process being so delicate that my mind was forced to focus on the task at hand and not on Peter. I was trying, and failing, to forget him.

I received a post card from my mother and father from Italy, a side trip they had included in their travels, describing the rich, creamy texture of gelato, in addition to the beautifully romantic canals of Venice, the historical baroque St. Peter's Cathedral in Rome, and the glorious hills of Tuscany. Mom was having the time of her life. Dad's wallet was stolen. I could just imagine Dad's enthusiasm to come back to the shop and get back to his comfort place. Yet I knew that Dad's greatest joy was making Mom happy. He just didn't quite know how to make himself relax when not in total control. I could never, ever tell Dad what I had done while he was away. I was his baby, and I had finally earned his trust to manage the shop. Yet I nearly brought a stranger into the loft, to live with me, a stranger almost twice my age. If Dad didn't kill me, he would surely kill Peter.

Peter. I wondered where he was and if he had found his home. I wondered if he was warm. When I was out, I would scan the streets in the off-chance that I would see him. Two nights had passed with temperatures falling to the forties, and as far as I could tell, he was gone--vanished into the great unknown.

I never told Julie that I didn't actually end the relationship as soon as she suggested. She was now developing her own life at the University of Idaho, a life that I was not part of. I didn't desire to run at the collegiate level; I never had the competitive drive that came so naturally to Julie. The jealous feelings had more to do with her constant activity. Julie had things to do, from morning until night. And because of this, we hardly spoke to each other. If I did call, she was with Corbin. I eventually stopped calling, not wanting to be a nuisance. She did call to remind me of her first college cross-country race at the university on Saturday. I promised her I would be there. The Art Walk on Friday night was going to exhaust me, but I do pride myself in keeping promises.

Donny was jittery, nonetheless, happy. "Are we ready to rip this joint up?" was his greeting, where I then proceeded to tell him that the Art Walk was an upscale event that I hired him for, and his vernacular needed to reflect that. I was praying to sell at least two Lenora originals, and hopefully recoup the spiraling profits Whitaker Jewelry was encountering this fall. The cherry blossom trees freshly strung with white Christmas lights created a beautiful setting for a lighthearted event, but business owners secretly served up warm smiles along with warm beverages in hopes of potential buyers, especially this year.

Donny dressed as I asked, in slacks and a dress shirt. However, I noticed his acne flared up again, and that he'd lost some weight. "Are you getting enough to eat at the bachelor pad?" I asked him coolly. "Open up the cheese and crackers. I'll go make the cider." I borrowed Mom and Dad's crock pot to make mulled cider. "Eat something if you're hungry, honestly."

"Where's the brandy?" Donny asked seriously.

"Hot cider. We can't serve wine or anything else when Dad's not here."

"Serve Toddy's and you'll sell more," Donny mused as he arranged the cheeses on a tray. He didn't take a bite. I went to the studio in back and retrieved about fifteen of my newest creations from the week. I displayed them in the middle right case. After years of observation, I have witnessed that the middle right case is where everyone stops to take a peek. The middle right case is always arranged with designs by Lenora.

After arranging the holiday snowflake pendants, diamond studded bangles, dove broaches, and ruby snowball earrings, I unlocked the doors. "Donny, would you go put something on the stereo?" I asked, as he was thumbing the cash in the register. "It's all been counted," I said, with a hint of warning. "Something festive," I suggested. "And for tonight, I just need you to stand behind the counter and take sales, and be charming."

116

Donny disappeared into the studio just as the door made its inaugural jingle. I grabbed a wedge to prop the door open, and noticed a very pale woman in a fuzzy, pink rabbit-hair beanie, her husband behind her. "Excuse me," I announced as I slipped by them and jammed the wedge in the door. I brushed her unusually thin arm as I bent down next to her. The gust of cold air swooshed into the shop, chilling me around the neck.

The man and woman were admiring the right middle shelf, the designs by Lenora, as predicted. "Donny, would you grab the patio heater while you're back there?" Just then, the music arrived, way too loud--Manheim Steamroller, and the woman gave a little jump and giggle. Her husband put his hand on the small of her back, gently holding her. "I'm sorry about that," and I offered them both some cider, in which they both declined. I noticed my broach, the one of the tree with the jewels, pinned to her scarf. In all my hustle and bustle to get the shop ready, I didn't notice the man who ordered the broach for his sick wife. Here she stood before me, pale, thin, and hairless.

I met the eyes of her husband, a warm thank you in his eyes. "I'm glad to see you like the broach," I said to the woman. "It's beautiful."

She looked at me with glossed-over eyes and smiled. "I wear it everyday," she spoke transparently.

She was weak, and small talk seemed immaterial. I didn't want to sound trite, but I continued, "You know, your husband brought in a picture of four very handsome young men. Lenora enjoyed the picture."

"They are good . . . kids." Her speech was slurred and her eyes were glassy, but she exuded an inner calm that only the dying know. Her husband's hand didn't leave her back, as if she could fall at any moment. She moved on in her own time.

Art Walkers started to trickle in steadily now, and I was busy greeting the town folk in front of the cases. I was approaching the point of sale with an out-of-towner, explaining the mystery of Lenora, when Donny's mood turned to melancholy, and I had to excuse myself to ask him to stop tapping the glass and act more professional. When I returned to the customer, she told me she would come back later after thinking through the purchase. With only one sale early in the evening, I determined to sell one more piece, even though the night was nearing its final hour.

I was using my best weapon, pulling out my bag of tricks to charm the pants off a group of past customers, friends of my parents. They inquired about Dad, and I told them about his romantic cruise with Mom, and they in turn had to boast about their most recent vacations to Fiji, China, and New Zealand. I aimed to seem interested, knowing that Dad always told me, "If they like you, they'll buy from you." This was part of the business that I didn't care too much for. I was in the midst of making my magic when Wyn slid quietly in the store, avoiding me and walking straight to Donny. As I kept up the small talk, I was eyeing Wyn and the heated discussion he was having with Donny. Donny sat behind the counter, apathetic to whatever Wyn was saying. Approaching Wyn from behind with her hands in her pockets was a blonde, a girl with a smile of pacifism on her face, the kind that is cute, but willing to please anyone, anytime.

"Have some cider, friend. Relax a bit," I overheard Donny say, which seemed to set Wyn off.

"I'm good until the end of the month. Then you'll need to look for someone else." Wyn's cheeks were flushed, and he turned and walked out with his date.

I excused myself from the group, who was now bragging of tropical seafood triumphs, crab-and-eel omelets. I followed Wyn out the door.

"Wyn!" I called, as he and the blonde were a few steps off. "Weren't you going to say 'hi'?"

"You looked a little busy," he said. The blonde eased up to him, as if they knew each other well. Wyn was uncomfortable, but introduced her anyway. "Maggie, this is Trish. Trish, Maggie."

I gave my most pleasant smile, and offered, "Hi, Trish. Wyn, can I talk to you for a moment?" He stepped aside, distancing himself out of earshot. The blonde walked toward the window display, giving her something to do during our awkward exclusion.

I felt a stab of jealousy, but downplayed it. "So I've been replaced?"

Wyn chuckled, more at his own thoughts than the words. "We're just friends."

"Really? Does *Trish* know that?"

Wyn looked at Trish, who was now tolerantly waiting. He turned back to me and admitted, "We'll see what happens. She's nice enough."

"All right," I smiled. "I was going to say, if it's okay with *Trish*, that I think I'm ready to end my running hiatus, if you want to join me."

"I don't think so," Wyn said softly, while looking down. "See you around, Whitaker," and Wyn put his hands in his jean pockets, walking down Sherman side by side with what appeared to be something new.

I dragged myself back into the shop, lacking my earlier eagerness to sell. Donny was apparently fired up after his confrontation with Wyn and was charming customers with newfound enthusiasm. He had a way of schmoozing when he had to, and at this moment he was completing a sale. I was grateful for my usually indolent cousin. I forgot to ask Wyn what the confrontation was about. I made a mental note to not get involved in other people's affairs, for once.

It was just past nine o'clock, and I thanked the last customers who were leaving, and pulled the heaters into the shop, the wedge out of the door, and locked up. Donny and I cleaned up the shop together, and I pulled fifty dollars out of the till. Three hours of pay, plus a tip. With what I just witnessed, I held some morsel of hope that maybe he was growing up, maybe we could actually go through this life with some amiable feelings toward each other. "Donny, would you be interested in picking up Dad and Mom from the airport with me on Sunday? I know they'd love to see you."

"I dunno, maybe," he replied casually. "Call me when you're ready to go."

He left the shop in a hurry, and I was left alone to close up the till. I counted the money three times, and realized that Donny had given himself a hefty bonus.

My mood turned sour. Donny had stolen from us, and it made a mockery of every aspiring feeling that I had started to rekindle toward him. I opened
120

the front door to leave, and turned so quickly in my anger that I dropped the keys which flew quickly onto the sidewalk. I muffled a curse, and then kicked the keys down the street.

A figure sitting on a nearby bench reached down and grabbed the keys. "I need those," I scolded the man, who was sitting with a hood over his head. "I need those back," I demanded. The man slowly handed them to me, and I grabbed them quickly and turned away without thanking him. I stopped in my tracks, and then slowly turned back to the man--to Peter, standing before me.

"Peter," I whispered, more to myself, confirming what I had imagined for days.

"I need a ride," he said coolly.

"A ride?" I questioned. "A ride to where?"

"To Wallace."

"Wallace?" Wallace was an hour up the interstate, the location of Peter's accident. Peter looked at me, dead serious.

"I can drive you to Wallace, I guess. It's the least I can do."

I drove him to Wallace that night with a billion questions I wanted to ask him, but not daring to break the silence. He was wearing new clothes, clothes that fit him better and cleaned him up a bit. He was clean shaven.

As we approached the historic mining town of Wallace, I was forced to break the silence. "First or second exit?" There were two exits, although the town didn't accommodate that kind of traffic or yardage. Since every single building downtown is on the National Registry of historic places, the interstate was redesigned to go over the city, instead of through it, hence an exit at either end of the interstate overpass.

Peter was silent, unsure. "Just take the first, I guess."

"Where are we heading?" I looked at Peter, and noticed intense recollection, eyebrows furrowed in deep concentration. He was reading every sign, looking down every alleyway, searching.

"Home," he said.

"You remember?" I asked, anxiously.

"I remember 23-D." He didn't peel his eyes off the passenger window, scanning through the darkness.

"23-D could be anywhere," I stated.

"There are less than a thousand people in this town. I know I can find it."

"Do you even know you're from Wallace? 23-D could be in Kellogg, Mullan, Post Falls, Sandpoint."

"It's Wallace. Turn here!" he demanded, as we approached a main drag on Cedar Street. With no traffic in sight, I turned and slowed the car to a crawl. We drove down Cedar until Peter asked me to stop. I pulled over and parked the car, illegally, in front of the Wallace Five & Dime. Peter got out and stood in front of the store, as I watched from inside. He put his palm onto his cheek, focusing, as if he were a forensic psychic leading police to a crime scene.

I got out of the car and stood by the driver's side, not wanting to get in his way but wondering what was going on. "I don't see a 23-D," I commented.

He then jetted into the road, crossed Cedar, and stopped suddenly at a brand-new park bench. He touched the bench and the plaque reading "In

Memory of ..." and started to walk quickly, pacing franticly down the street, through a dark alley. I followed him, ten paces back, until he disappeared around the corner. When I rounded the corner, I was overwhelmed with the dirty amber glow from the group of derelict apartment lights, six in all. Dead mosquitoes and flies and dust gathered on the front-porch lights. And although they looked abandoned, there were lights on in two of the six studio apartments. Peter stood in front of the corner floor unit, a 23-D in rusty brass on the front door. I watched, still ten paces back, as Peter grabbed the door handle, twisting it ever so gently. The door squeaked open, and I could see that three lights were now on in the apartments in the alley. I stood there for a long time, not sure if I should leave or stay. Ten minutes passed, and Peter reemerged from door 23-D, calm on his previously frantic face. "Want to come in?"

I smiled, my hands hidden in my pockets. I fumbled an awkward reply, "No, I shouldn't. I've got to get home."

"Let me make you a cup of coffee, M. I won't bite." He was persistent, and inviting. I was easily won over.

Peter definitely led a simple life. No TV, no stereo, no decor of any sort; nothing that makes a house a home. White walls, a twin bed with what looked like car blankets, and a small kitchenette with a table and two chairs. While Peter rummaged through the cupboards, pulling money out of a coffee tin, I took in the place, looking for clues as to who he was. There was a terrible stench in the studio, not of rotting food, but a staleness of windows that hadn't been opened in a long time. I noticed a pair of jeans and a brown tee shirt folded neatly on his bed. Peter followed my eyes to his folded clothing and picked them up to put them away. Underneath was a laptop computer. Peter's eyes widened at the discovery, and a sense of victory filled him.

"I was going to wear these. I was dirty, just off the mountain. I was going to wear these." He stopped, reaching for his face. "I needed to shave." He again gripped his jaw, feeling the absence of his beard. "I had to go to the Five & Dime to get soap, and that's all I remember."

"You were hit by a car," I reminded him. "They thought you were homeless."

"I was just off the mountain," he repeated.

"What were you on the mountain for? Do you remember?"

He thought about it, nodding in recollection. He sat on his bed and opened up his laptop. He powered it up, and the automatic wallpaper was of a gray wolf. "Wolves. The Rocky Mountain Gray Wolves that were reintroduced in the mid nineties. I study them." Upon connecting to the internet, his homepage of the U.S. Fish & Wildlife logo appeared. He was standing on the precipice of rediscovering himself. He stopped from diving into more research, research he wanted or needed to do alone. He stood up, approached me as if he wanted to hug me, yet held back and offered a handshake. "Thanks for the ride, Margaret." It was his way of saying 'you can go now.' He must have forgotten about the coffee.

"You're welcome." I walked toward his door, not wanting this to be goodbye, not this abruptly. I teetered on walking out, but found the nerve to ask one final question. "Where were you these last few days?"

He looked at me, deciding if he was going to include me in the details of his life. The silence was unusually long--another boundary that I had no right to cross. "Never mind, I'll go." I tried to sound chipper, but my tone was anything but.

I walked out the door. I stood outside for a moment, wanting answers, and frustrated that I couldn't get them. Knowing there was nothing else I could do, I walked down the alley in the cold, foggy night.

"Margaret!" Peter was standing in his doorway. "Will you let me answer your question?"

He invited me in, again, and I was keenly aware of our age difference now. I felt like a child; my immaturity was suddenly obvious, although I had done everything to disguise it. Peter walked over to his laptop, closing it suddenly. "Have a seat," he suggested, and I sat on the end of his bed. "How about at the table," he offered, casually.

He had a little, round wooden table with two chairs, centimeters from the kitchen, about ten steps from his bed. I sat down quickly, as he rummaged through the cupboards, looking for cups.

As he found a pot to boil water in, he started to answer my question. "I live by one principle: Trust yourself and nobody else. But I trusted you. I had to. I couldn't remember anything, except my name and the number on this door." He paused, stirring the coffees and handing me one. Then Peter leaned against the wall, not joining me at the table. "I walked a long way, maybe ten miles that day. I walked through the city, up and down streets, looking for anything that would jar my memory. I hoped that I would recognize someone I knew, or someone would recognize me. I sat in the park and slept under a tree the first night--worst night of my life."

"Because you were cold?"

Peter looked at me and then muffled a bitter laugh. "Because I was disappointed--"

"Disappointed?" His confession was hard to hear, knowing full well that because of me, Peter was homeless. If I hadn't gotten involved, he would have been placed somewhere safe, somewhere warm where he could have more time to remember.

"--disappointed that I wasn't going home with you, that you were nineteen, that the life I was trying so hard to remember wasn't my life at all." Peter stared at his coffee, as I tried to sip the black acrid stuff.

"I'm sorry," I whispered while warming my hands on the coffee mug.

"Are you, because that's what I can't figure out? Are you really sorry, or was I a little project for you, something to make you feel good, a charity case?" His voice was rising, hostility in every word.

"You weren't a project."

"Then what? What's in it for a teenager to claim to be a fiancé to a stranger, a grown man? Tell me that!"

"I *wasn't* thinking. I wasn't thinking about age or manipulating anyone. I just . . ." my emotions got the worst of me, and I couldn't look at him anymore. "You were alone. And maybe my biggest flaw is that I try to save people. I wanted to save you."

"You were fulfilling your own needs that night." Peter said it, directly to me, the one truth I didn't want to acknowledge. "Admit it. You did it for *you*." He was not the slightest bit wavering on this point.

126

He didn't want to accept my justification; he wanted the bare truth. "Admit it!"

"Okay. You're right. I did it for me." Shame encompassed me. I was demoralized, terrified of what would come next.

Peter looked at me for a long while, coldly staring into my frightened eyes, until I finally had the nerve to look up. He cracked a smile in the corner of his closed lips. "That is the first honest thing I've heard you say." He chuckled under his breath. "You're a kid, just a kid." He shook his head, "Don't get messed up in stuff like this."

I nodded, point well-taken. For a moment, he seemed to be offering peace, his smile an affirmation that he had forgiven me. But I couldn't resist the one comment that changed everything.

Chapter Nine: Wake-Up Call

"I don't regret it." I said. "I don't regret the lie."
Peter's demeanor went from calm to tense,
instantly. "I don't regret it, because you survived,
you made it, and I got to be there when no one else
would have been. If it means admitting I'm selfish,
I admit it--but you're alive."

Peter hovered on the subtext behind my words.
We had been through near death and then new life
together, a bonding experience that outweighs the
partition of age. We loved each other then, though
under false pretense, and now I had the courage to
justify my actions.

He slammed his coffee cup down, dark liquid
sloshing onto the kitchen countertop. He grabbed
his head with both palms, cradling his temples.
Peter stammered over to his bed, crumbling
downward as if he had just been hit. I stared at
him, aghast at his impulsive overreaction. I
watched on, as he curled in his bed, still holding
his head. Suddenly I knew this wasn't an
overreaction at all. I rushed to his side.

"Where are your pills?" He didn't respond, and
I knew the answer: He had none. Of course he had
none. I had kicked him onto the streets before
filling his prescriptions. "Oh, geez, you don't have
any, do you? Where's the prescription?"

"It's going away," he breathed between words, dodging my last question.

"I'll go fill your prescription."

"Don't," he demanded. "You have done enough. It's going away." Peter sat up, reaffirming, "I'm good."

I *had* done enough. And now I was meddling in his life. I stood up and pulled the car keys out of my pocket. "You know, you never did answer my one question," I said, and walked toward the door. Peter looked at me, trying to remember what my original question was. "Where did you go?" I reminded him.

"A shelter," was all he said, numbly.

Peter stood up slowly, took a breath, and followed me out the door to my car on Cedar Street. I unlocked the car door, wanting to cry my eyes out but staying strong enough to not appear more immature than I already felt. All the nervous energy built up in me presented itself like an anthill that got disturbed by a meddling stick. "Are you sure I can't fill that prescription?"

"No," he nearly whispered.

"Okay," I whispered back. "Goodbye, then." I wanted to throw my arms around him, but I slipped into my car, shutting the door quickly. He stood next to my window, taking in the precocious young woman who had just complicated his world. In a daze, he glared at me somberly as I drove away that night, another long hour on the interstate to get home.

As confused and emotional as I was, the lack of sleep caught up with me, and I was subtly aware of the burning in my dry, tired eyes. I rolled down the window, turned on the air conditioner, and pumped the stereo bass loud--anything to keep me from drifting off during the midnight drive home. I thought of Peter in the shelter. That explained his new clothes and clean-shaven appearance. Secretly, I felt relieved that he found a shelter. If Peter had remained John Doe and survived, the hospital would have transitioned him to a shelter eventually.

When I finally reached my loft, it was all I could do to key myself in and collapse on my bed. I had just barely closed my eyes when my phone woke me up from the deepest of sleep.

"This is your wake-up call," Julie announced cheerfully.

"What?" I mumbled.

"The gun goes off at nine. You said you'd be there."

"Your meet. I was out really, really late, Jules."

"You promised."

Despite my exhaustion, I did promise to watch her first college cross-country meet, which I missed. This was her last home meet. "All right, I'll be there." I hung up the phone and snuggled under the covers in frustration. I skipped the shower and went straight to jeans, a jacket and sneakers.

The University of Idaho has a great course for spectators. The 5-kilometer run wound all through a hilly, green golf course. I stood on a grassy knoll and watched from afar as the runners lined up. The bang of the gun announced the start, and Julie, who had been our lead runner at Coeur d'Alene High, was a freshman runner with nerves. She started out in the middle of the pack, and worked her way up to about tenth place until she faltered back again. I looked on, devoid of feelings. Julie crossed the finish line as the fourth runner from the University of Idaho, collapsing into the arms of her new teammates, leaning on them like I used to lean on her. This is the first time I had seen Julie not win. I wanted to go congratulate her, but I turned toward the parking lot, got in my car, and drove home.

Chapter Ten: Tranquilize

I worked diligently the rest of Saturday, morning to night, knowing that Mom and Dad were due home the following morning. When it was time, I drove to the airport alone--Donny was unreachable--and returned with Mom and Dad completely unaware of what had transpired during their absence. I was afraid they would never trust me and, consequently, Dad would never retire.

I dropped Mom and Dad off at home, and visited briefly until it was obvious jet lag had consumed them. I bid them good night and told Dad I would see him at the shop in the morning.

I knew that a few things were not in order, so I decided to key myself into the shop and clean, file some papers, and prepare for a normal transition with Dad returning. The answering machine had three messages: One from hospital accounting, one from Dr. James, and one from Mira. All had the same foreboding inquiry and threat: Who are you, and charges will be filed.

I felt weak and nauseated, and I wasn't sure if I was more embarrassed or mortified. I erased the messages before driving straight to the hospital.

Accounting was closed, which I didn't even consider since it was eight o'clock on Sunday night. I could try back at nine in the morning, but that would leave Dad to wonder why I wasn't at the shop. I took a breath and put on my fake badge one last time, crossing the double doors to the neuro unit. I was sure Mira wouldn't be working the night shift, but I could leave her a note with my cellular phone number so she wouldn't call the shop anymore. Dr. James came out of a room and looked straight at me.

"Margaret?" he inquired, suspiciously.

"I came to clear up a few things. I wanted to give you my cell number, since the messages were left on my business machine."

"Peter's been in for physical therapy, and he has remembered his last name, which isn't Jackson."

"Right."

"Do you know what his last name is?" Dr. James barely took a moment to breathe, and continued, "Of course you don't, because you don't know him. You had no right to be here, to sign legal documents--"

I interrupted him, "I know."

"Peter can report this, as I've advised, and take legal action. You have violated his privacy, his safety, and the security of this hospital."

Violated. It was a strong word, but true. Even beyond violating his privacy, I knew I had been there for him while he recovered, and I'm not sure I would choose otherwise even at this moment. "I don't expect anyone to understand, but I've explained myself to Peter and he knows the truth."

"My god, you're just a kid." Dr. James softened, just a bit. "It's Florence Nightingale Syndrome, where caretakers fall in love with their vulnerable patients."

I was trying not to be belittled. "Peter understands. He's letting it go."

"Apparently, he does. However, I can't. This is my department. I am responsible for the welfare of these patients, not just for their health and recovery, but for their security. You violated his security and our trust. Maybe Peter won't press charges, but as a physician, I will."

"Dr. James, please. If you give me the chance to explain--"

"Accounting has been following a ghost trail trying to collect on a fictitious person, and they, too, are pressing charges of medical fraud. And Mira, I think she is--" Dr. James paused at the mention of Mira, "she is hurt. To know you have fooled us and our patient doesn't bode well with anyone, especially her."

A small morsel of courage appeared, and as overwhelmed as I was, I couldn't avoid the truth. "I am truly sorry for the deception I've forced onto your department, and I will do whatever it takes to make this right. I made a mistake, a terrible lapse in judgment. I wanted to help him, because he was alone. I knew it was wrong, but for one moment, and because of the end results, it was right."

"It was never right, Mira!" Dr. James seethed. "Margaret," he corrected himself. In his fluster, he looked to the ground and calmly excused himself.

I never got the tongue-lashing I expected from Mira. My cell phone never rang, and all threats of impending lawsuits vanished. Eventually, the sound of my cell phone ringing didn't cause me to run to a hidden corner to answer in privacy. What I didn't know was that Dr. James had covered for me, explaining to accounting that Peter's mistaken last name was a clerical error due to poor communication, and that I had come in to rectify the situation. Dr. James was giving out his own little measure of forgiveness. And although the incident was a clean case, now practically incognito and undone, I had never felt more depressed. My life, for the first time, lacked purpose, motivation, and excitement. I had tasted a thrill and was struggling to enjoy creating art when the intrigue--the inspiration that kept me up night after night--was gone.

October turned into November, and the leaves had nearly all fallen, leaving the city barren and cold. I worked every day with my father, the quietness in the shop a safe place to hide my pain. Thanksgiving Day arrived, and I couldn't hide my depression from my mom. After our usual feast I joined my mother in the kitchen to hand-wash the fine china. This gave her the perfect opportunity to ask in private if I was happy working at the shop.

"Of course," I said.

"Mags, I know that you insist on working to help me out," my father said from behind, and suddenly I felt like I had just stepped into an intervention. "We want you to have your time--time to be a kid--go discover yourself."

"What does that mean, to discover yourself? I already know who I am and what I want." I was feeling trapped.

"We want you to go to college, Mags," Mom said. I rolled my eyes.

"What does Holden's teacher tell him," my father said, "in *Catcher In the Rye?* What does his teacher tell him to do, his favorite teacher after he flunks out of private school?"

"To develop his mind," I answered.

"Yes!" Dad was getting excited. "To see how far he could develop his mind."

"I don't need to go to college." I could see my mother biting her tongue, as we had gone round and round about the whole college thing for the last year and a half.

"I think you may, because you're not happy here." Dad was looking at me, demanding an answer.

"I'm happy," I lied.

"You mope around the shop. You've stopped running. You never go out. In the shop, you're invisible."

"I'm tired. Plus, you know how winters are here."

Dad had an intensity that was uncharacteristic of him. He put down the pot that he started drying and looked directly through me. "Damn it, Margaret. Be straight with me! I've lost one daughter, and I don't intend to lose another. You are *not* okay, and I want to know why."

"I have the right to privacy," I sassed.

"Like hell you do. Are you taking anything, because if Donny--"

"Come on!" This was incredulous.

"Then what is it? Is it a boy?"

I let out a sigh of frustration, "Not exactly a boy."

Dad's eyes popped, then Mom's. They both slowly turned to each other, as if finally seeing the hidden lining, yet completely misreading the situation. Mom reached for a china salad plate to dry. "I see," was all she could mumble.

"Could it be an experimental phase, because with artists it's not unusual to feel a wide gamut ... a continuum ...

"Wait a second. What are you implying?"

"You said it's not a boy."

136

"I met a *man*, not a boy. He doesn't feel for me. The end. So if I'm moping, forgive me."

Mom shot dad a dangerous look, warning him to back off, but also revealing the relief in her eyes. And then, in her nurturing way, she put her arm around my back, rubbing it like she did when I was thirteen.

"Is there anything I can do for you, Honey?" Mom asked.

"Not this. Actually, you *can* do something. Don't mention him. I need to forget him, and I'm having a hard time doing that."

Mom looked worried. "It seems pretty intense. Talking about it can be helpful."

"No."

"All right, we won't talk about him. I know what will help: fireworks."

The annual Coeur d'Alene Thanksgiving parade and town fireworks show was a possible distraction, as there would be several thousand locals lining the downtown streets in festive merriment. I had enthusiastically gone to the parade every year with Mom, but this year I had to force myself to go.

After the dishes were dried, we bundled up in scarves, mittens, hats, and our thickest jackets, and Mom and I walked ten blocks to Sherman Avenue. We stood outside Whitaker Jewelry, watching the floats parade by, while making small talk with patrons who recognized us. I spotted a few kids from the high school marching band, along with cheerleaders out braving the cold. The Humane Society float moseyed on by, with canines wagging their tails adorned in Santa hats. Various church groups created musical floats and depictions of the Christ child, all being pulled on someone's backyard trailer. The local mayor waved at her citizens, the National Guard Reservists marched, and I watched on as small children held out their hands for any morsels of candy that would be passed out by clowns. As the last of the three separate Santa Clauses went by, I spotted Wyn across the street, and when he looked our way, I gave a little wave. Wyn was with the blonde, who didn't see me or the slight wave that Wyn gave back.

Mom noticed this interaction and smiled, and I realized her smile was misguided. I didn't correct her, or clarify that Wyn was not the object of my aching heart.

After the fire department ended the parade, the crowds followed into the street to walk down Sherman Avenue toward Independence Point to get a lakeside view of the fireworks. We found an area to stand, and within moments Mom ran into an old acquaintance and was recounting her European highlights. I stood in the cold, dark night, amidst thousands of people. There were couples hand in hand, children in snowsuits braving the now single-digit weather, teenagers wrestling in the flirtatious way that they do, and others smoking, drinking coffee, and aimlessly fiddling with cell phones.

And there he was, sitting on the curb--Peter-- dressed in a navy blue vest and long-sleeve shirt, jeans and hiking boots. He was standing about 50 yards in front of where we were standing, just staring at the lake. He was alone, unaware that I was behind him.

I wanted to ask him how he's doing, and yet I couldn't. He was a free man, and I had to accept that. The first of the fireworks started, and I averted my eyes to the sky, while Manheim Steamroller played its energetic Christmas vibes with the sky exploding in colors. Mom had returned and I smiled at her, the first smile in a while. When the show was over, I turned my back on the lake and on Peter, put my arm in Mom's, and walked home with her. The length of the ten blocks took us twice as long to return as it did to arrive, as the crowds bottlenecked before dispersing, but my spirit slowly rose as I willingly walked away from Peter, choosing not to interfere with fate. Once in Mom's driveway, I hugged her goodbye and retrieved my car and drove back to my loft. My parking space next to the dumpster was taken with parade parking, and I had to park in front near Whitaker Jewelry, now that they had opened up Sherman Avenue again. After locking my car, I noticed a figure sitting on the bench across the street. He stood up and jetted across the street toward me. "Margaret!" he called. It was Peter, in the same blue vest and tee shirt.

"You didn't look before crossing," I pointed out.

"Sure I did," he smiled.

"No, you didn't." I put my hands in my pockets, as I noticed his bare hands were buried deep in his. "And if you get hit by a pizza deliverer, I won't be visiting you in the hospital this time."

Peter laughed, "Fair enough." He was at ease. My jaw started to chatter. He continued, "I had physical therapy at the hospital today and stayed for Thanksgiving dinner, yellow tray included. After hearing how much you have affected Mira, Dr. James, and the other staff members, I realized that I needed to officially *thank you.*"

"They advised you to press charges against me--criminal charges," I reminded him.

"I should have died. The percentages of people who survive similar traumatic brain injuries are low, and I should have been one of them. Your arrival was the day I started to recover. Everyone knows that."

I downplayed his explanation, "That's kind, but you did it. You're the survivor."

"I'm alive because of you." Peter was adamant.

"I lied, Peter. I deceived people. I deceived myself by convincing myself I was there for you. I was wrong."

"I came to the parade tonight, because of you. I don't do parades." He was shivering with just his vest on in the frigid air, but he was looking me in the eyes for the first time. "It's Thanksgiving, and I just came to say *thanks*."

Peter was giving me permission to live with myself, to forgive myself, and to believe that I actually did something honorable. Humbled, yet slightly confused, I whispered, "Okay." We stared at each other, the cold air allowing us to see our breath.

"Would you like to go for a cup of coffee?" Peter asked out of the blue. "It's Thanksgiving, and it's damn cold."

I was shocked, unsure how the tables had turned so quickly. And even more so, I was equally shocked at my truthful response, "I don't drink coffee."

Peter smirked, "You don't?"

"There's a lot you don't know about me," I laughed at myself, finally admitting the truth. "Orange juice. I drink orange juice, or hot chocolate."

The connection that I knew I had felt all along was raw, palpable in this moment, that is, until the shadow in Whitaker Jewelry caught our eyes. We both turned, streamlining our attention to the store. The shop was still--not a thing out of line. Peter walked toward the corner, which only revealed a desolate alley.

"You'll go crazy if you chase every shadow. That is one of the first things I had to get over when I moved downtown," I confessed.

Peter looked at me, then back over his shoulder. His arms were shaking, as he couldn't stop the tremors in the cold. "You don't need coffee. You need a complete thawing out. Do you want to come in, just to warm up? I've got . . . hot chocolate."

He shivered, "I don't mean to impose."

"Trust me, you're not imposing." I assured myself that this time I knew the boundaries.

Inside, I turned up the thermostat, gave him a blanket that he wrapped around his shoulders, and poured water in the kettle before putting it on the stove. Peter looked around my tiny apartment at pictures I had on the wall. I chattered away, nervously. "My parents were away on a six-week cruise when I met you. They don't know anything, and it's probably the one and only secret I have from them. It would kill my dad, who sees me as-- how do I put it--angelic." He saw the framed photo that Mira had taken of us in the hospital and was staring at it. "Oh geez." I went and took the photo off the wall, putting it face down on the table. "Stupid, I know." Then, to change the subject, I reached for a diversion. "How's physical therapy going?"

Peter seemed aloof, but eventually answered my question. "I have occasional dizzy spells and some other awkward side effects, but I'm back to work, and that's all that matters to me."

"The wolf thing?"

"The wolf thing. Back on site, tomorrow actually." You could see the anticipation in his eyes.

"What site?" I asked.

"I work a field study in the Clearwater National Forest. I'm heading to sites 7 and 8 tomorrow to retrieve data, way the heck out in nowhere."

"Who do you work for?" I asked.

"Both Idaho and Montana state agencies, as well as the feds, to provide third-party research on the reintroduced wolves. The feds want to protect them if need be, under the Endangered Species Act. The states want to hunt them, if they are growing, and bring in revenue to the states and stabilization for the species. I present the research. They make the decisions."

"You're a wolf biologist." I was fascinated, but still didn't grasp his job fully. "How do you study wolves?"

"I have camera sites located in the mountains southeast of Wallace, and I track them, watch them, and mostly film them. Sometimes it's by foot, sometimes by air. Most of my wolves are tagged."

"You're undercover?" I asked.

Peter nodded. "I need to get the data out of the cameras and reload them--study them. I leave first thing in the morning."

"Aren't they dangerous, the wolves?" I still couldn't believe that people do this, that *he* does this.

"The wolves aren't the primary danger, being alone is. Anything can happen out there." Peter could sense he was worrying me, as I was wrapping my brain around his job. "It's what I live for. I'm safe out there, trust me."

"And yet you get hit by a car?"

He looked at me and smiled.

The kettle was now singing and I poured two cups of hot chocolate. I handed Peter a mug, and he warmed his hands on it. I could feel him looking at me with the same intensity and unexplainable connection that I was trying to hide.

"I'd like to see your work one day. The jewelry," he broke the ice.

I hesitated, before confessing, "I've got a piece that I created when you were sick, sort of inspired by you. I'd really like you to see it."

Peter stared at his hot chocolate, before drinking a few gulps. "That's nice, Margaret." He stood up slowly, "I'd love to see it, another time. I should be going."

"Don't go. Stay. We can just talk, some more. I like your company." I stood up, desperate for him to stay.

Peter took a long breath, and stood still. "Look, M. You are sweet." He looked at me with eyes that revealed conflicted desire.

"Don't say it. Don't say that I am too young. I already know that. Just don't say it."

He looked at me, deadpan. He pulled me in to his chest and gave me a warm embrace, a bear hug like that of a big brother. "We've been through a lot together, you and I," Peter admitted, and I knew that our bond had never been broken since the moment it formed in the hospital. "That connection runs pretty deep."

"I want to go with you," I said, "to see the wolves." My heart was through my chest, and I stood silently still, not sure what would happen next. I waited, and he brushed my hair out of my eyes, while looking beyond me. He looked confused, then alarmed. He cocked his head slightly, just before we both heard glass shattering in the shop below.

I stood there, frozen, listening to shoes stepping on glass, everything in my head jumbled. Peter was gone. I scurried down the stairs with my bear spray in hand. I went to unbolt the passage to the shop from the bottom of the stairs and found the door ajar. This meant that the silent alarm was going off, and the police would be here soon. I'm not sure what I was expecting to find, but in all reality, I was unequipped to face a thief, someone grabbing for the jewels that the store so prominently displayed. Dad always told me to stay put and wait for the police if anything like this were to happen. A sudden whizzing sound, *zipft*, was all I could make out, and then a low moan, and a thud to the floor. More scrambling and then, "Let's get out of here!" More scuffling, and by instinct, I inched around the door frame to peek at what was happening. What I found was unmistakable--Peter was standing inches inside the door, gun drawn, with Donny motionless on the floor, blood trickling from his hands while his eyes were glazed open. Peter had shot Donny.

"Oh god!" was all I could say. "Donny!"

Peter stepped over Donny--impassive--and searched beyond the front door, which was ajar. The only witness to the crime appeared to be the dark, silent street. Peter shut the front door and bolted it. He held a band of cut wires in his hand, tampered with by Donny, who was dead for all I knew.

"Peter, what did you do?" I cried in fear.

"You know him?" Peter asked, feverishly.

"He's my cousin. He's just a kid."

"He'll wake up in about thirty minutes." Peter was looking at his tranquilizer gun, and put it back in his pocket. Donny let out a sigh, heavily dozed, but a wonderful sigh nonetheless. "I am not supposed to use this on humans. I just violated the . . ." and he couldn't finish his sentence, as he began to walk out the back exit. "I've got to go."

I felt for Donny's pulse, and was assured that he would be okay. A bulging pocketknife slipped out of his breast pocket, along with wire clippers and a small Philips screwdriver. Donny was armed.

"Peter!" I called out the back door, "Don't leave," I pleaded. His shadow stopped, and I felt his presence. "Please stay," I whispered, as tears were now streaming down my cheeks. The shop was broken into, Donny was lying helpless on the floor, and I didn't know what to do next.

Peter was shaking. "I can't use this on people," he confessed. "It just happened."

"I know. It's okay," I reminded him. I was using a cloth to wipe off Donny's hands, which were covered in blood. Clutched in his hands were several bloodied diamond rings. Those wouldn't cut him, but I now recognized the source, a broken glass case. When Donny cut the security wire, he cut an electrical wire as well, disenabling the metal casing grids to release out of the glass fully. The only way to the jewelry was through the glass. I asked Peter to carry Donny up to my loft before we created a scene from outside. We carried him up the stairs to my bed. I cleaned up his hands and wrapped them in a hand towel.

Once Donny was situated, I turned to Peter, who was standing back and restless.

"You were just protecting me," I assured him.

Peter bit his lip, and I could tell he was unsure. Donny started to stir, and Peter began tensing up again. "Forgive me, Margaret. I shouldn't have--I've got to go." Peter headed toward my door.

"Wait! I want to come with you tomorrow, to your research."

He shook his head, "Why? It's not a good idea."

"One time. Let me come one time. I can handle it."

Peter paused at the threshold, and said under his breath, "It's not safe, Margaret."

"What time are you leaving?" I can be very persistent.

Peter looked me straight in the eyes and said, "6 a.m."

"I'll be there at five-thirty," I stated matter-of-factly.

Peter's head shook no, but his jade-green eyes said yes. He turned and left quickly.

My heart wanted to sing, but my simple joy was quickly returned to concern, as Donny was regaining consciousness. His eyes were fluttering, yet he wasn't able to focus. I sat next to Donny, angrier than hell that he put our family through this, and angry that he'd ruined a magical moment and turned it into tragedy. Yet, as he lay in my bed, stirring with bandaged hands and a decent bruise on his left cheekbone, I saw a helpless, lost child. I sat on the edge of the bed and stroked his hair, forgiving him for wrecking everything, because he was Donny.

I awoke Dad from a deep sleep and told him the bare minimum of the story over the phone: There was a break-in, and the alarm was deactivated so no police were involved, but Donny was. Dad arrived with Mom, ten minutes later.

Chapter Eleven: I'm Going

When Donny came to, Mom and I were sitting at the foot of the bed, wondering if he would wake peacefully or if he would try to bolt. Dad was downstairs in the shop, cleaning the glass and blood off the floor and taking an inventory of missing items. I briefly told them about the man I had fallen for, Peter, his work with the wolves, and the illegal use of his tranquilizer. I omitted how we met.

Grateful for Peter's protection, Dad was unsure how to proceed, knowing that calling the police would not only compromise Peter's job, but also the well-being of his grandson, Donny. I called Wyn and asked him to come give Donny a ride home. I recalled that hostility between Wyn and Donny at the Art Walk, and now saw the storm brewing. I should have called Dawn, to tell her about her son's troubles. But I couldn't come up with one good reason of how Dawn's involvement could possibly make anything better.

"Mom, do you think we should go get Dad?" I asked, as Donny was now sitting up, dazed, looking rather annoyed while wildly scoping out the room with his head flopping from side to side.

"Who's here?" he kept demanding, as if in a drunken stupor. "Get out, get out of here!"

"I don't want to leave you alone," Mom hesitated. Time was of the essence.

"I'll be okay. Go get Dad," I demanded, a little more bossy than I intended. If there was one person in the family that Donny wasn't threatened by, it was me.

Mom scurried down the stairs and into the shop hallway.

Donny stood up out of bed, threw the bloody towels on the floor, and bent his neck slightly, wincing at the sore spot on his neck where the dart had hit. "What the hell!" he moaned as he caressed his neck, and bolted past me toward the door, then lost his balance and swaggered into the wall.

I reached for his elbow. "Donny, let me help you. You're not going to feel right for a while," I advised him, while pulling him back to bed.

Donny pushed me against the wall, a rage in him I've never seen before. I was more stunned by the realization that I, too, was thrown aside by him than by my head hitting the wall.

Then it happened, fast as lightning. Donny was mauled by a fierce figure, literally lifted off the ground and thrown back onto my bed, pounced upon and restrained by Wyn, who had just reached the top of the stairs. "You son of a bitch!" Wyn cursed at him. "You son of a bitch!" Wyn said, over and over. Donny attempted to fight back, with no strength to aid him. Wyn was breathing hard, adrenaline fueling the fire. Donny cursed some more, giving in with each evasive attempt, until Dad arrived, prying Wyn off of Donny.

Donny gingerly sat up, and pushed himself up off the bed. Dad stood in his way. "Sit down, Donny." Donny stared him right in the face, nose to nose, and refused to sit. Dad continued. "Sit down, and I won't call the cops. Can you do that? Can we not get the authorities involved?" Donny looked at him with hatred in his eyes. "Sit down, now." Dad was firm. "Who was with you, in the shop?" Dad interrogated.

"No one." Donny was not going to cooperate.

"Where are they?" Dad insisted.

"Nowhere."

"What are you on?" Dad was fierce.

"Tranquilizers," and then Donny laughed. No one else did.

"Wyn?" Dad was staring at Donny, no one else.

"Methamphetamines," Wyn whispered under his breath.

"Meth," Dad repeated, and then took in a deep breath. "Why?" Dad was shaking his head, in disgust.

"Why not?" Donny answered angrily. "You should try it."

This was not Donny. He was lazy, sure. However, he had a respectful reverence for my dad, his grandfather. This was not Donny.

"Son, I'm going to give you one last chance to be straight with me, or else you leave me no choice but to call the police. Let Grandma and I take you home with us, and we'll figure this out. It's your choice, Donny."

"Get out of my way, old man." Donny stood up, winced at his hand as it was still bleeding, wiping it on his jeans.

Wyn stepped in, blocking his way out the door. "You need help, man. This is your family!"

Donny turned to look at all of us standing there, and then laughed, as if the joke was on us.

He looked at my dad, then me, and ran out into the darkness.

I never thought I would see my father do it, the compassionate, savior of the family. He opened his cell phone and spoke quietly into the receiver, "Yes, I'd like to report a robbery. Whitaker Jewelry. The suspect just fled the scene."

The picture of my happy little life was being chiseled away moment by moment. Donny was an addict, and now a criminal.

Dad was calm yet calculating his next move. "I'm going down to the shop. The police will want a description."

"How can I help, Mr. Whitaker?" Wyn asked.

"You can't, son. I'm sorry you've had to put up with him this long. I truly am. I should have seen the signs a long time ago." Dad paused, heaviness in his eyes. "You should go home." And then he realized that sending Wyn home to Donny's rental would not be ideal. "Wyn, you're welcome to stay at our place tonight. Maggie, you should come home too, for now."

"He can stay here," I said, and I tossed a pillow on the couch, gesturing his makeshift bed. "I want to stay here. I'll be fine, Dad."

"I'll call my parents in the morning. I'll move back home with them. Sorry about the short notice," Wyn said to Dad, his landlord.

"No, I'm sorry." At that, Dad went downstairs to file the report with the police, who had now arrived.

Mom stripped my bedsheets, which were streaked with Donny's blood. "I'll take this home and work on the stains." Mom wrapped her arms around me, and I could feel her holding me up as if every inch of my being wanted to collapse into a puddle on the floor.

"Mom, what's going to happen to him?" I whispered through tears.

"Donny will have to face the fire. It's the only way."

"Not Donny--Peter."

I saw Wyn look away, and then he ducked into my tiny kitchen.

"I don't know," she admitted. "What happened, happened."

"Dad can't report this. Nobody has to say anything about Peter using his gun."

"What is this man doing in your loft, with a tranquilizer gun? Please explain to me." Mom looked frightened, even more so, angry.

"He works with the wolves. He's a field biologist. It looks bad, but he's good, Mom. He's a very good person, and he was only trying to protect me and the shop. Dad can't reveal this."

"We don't lie. If it comes up, Dad will tell the truth." Mom looked at me, absorbing the passion she could see in my eyes. "This is the older man." I nodded. "How much older, Maggie?"

"Older. Does it matter?"

"It could."

"He's a good person. He's kind. He's--"

"How old?" Mom persisted.

"Thirty-two," I whispered.

"Margaret Claire! You're nineteen years old!"

"So! At what age am I grown up, eighteen, or twenty-one, or thirty? At what age am I an adult, in your eyes? He's right for me."

"There's something very wrong with a thirty-two-year-old man who pursues a teenager," she refuted.

152

"He's not pursuing me." I admitted. "But he feels it--I know he does."

"Maybe at thirty-two he has more insight than you do. Have you thought of that? He won't pursue you for a reason, thank God."

Realizing that the conversation was going in circles, I knew I had to get back to my main concern. "Mom, please tell Dad not to mention the tranquilizer gun. Please, I'm begging you. He'll lose his job; he'll lose everything he's got."

Wyn came around the corner with two cups of hot cocoa. The tension was thick in the room, and he immediately retreated back into the kitchen. Mom saw this gesture and found his entrance a great place for her exit. "Wyn, come on in, Dear." He cautiously came around the corner, offering a mug to Mom. She refused, saying she needed to join Dad downstairs. "We'll lock up behind us, Margaret." And then, to Wyn, "Thank you for staying here tonight. It makes me feel better to know you'll stay with Margaret tonight."

Wyn nodded, as he stood between our tensions.

Mom started to leave, but I knew there was one thing I must be truthful about. "Mom, I'm going to see him tomorrow. I'm going to Wallace in the morning, and I'm going to travel into the field with him, to study the wolves. I wanted you to hear it from me. I won't be at work for a few days. Please tell Dad not to worry."

"Absolutely not. You can't go, Margaret. I won't let you do this."

"I'm nineteen. I'm going." Mom bit her lip. I could see her chest rise slowly. She turned toward the stairs, her back facing me, and said, "Goodnight, Margaret. I love you," and she left.

Wyn was still standing, holding the cups of cocoa, wide-eyed.

"Sit." I declared, as I repositioned a bed pillow on the couch. He sat, and I sat opposite him. "Do *not* lecture me, Wyn."

Wyn sat, staring at me with a wicked smile. "You're crazy."

"I said don't lecture me." I snarled.

"Just an observation," he said, innocent enough.

"I'm sorry you had to get involved in the Whitaker family drama."

"Don't think you're so special. Everyone has drama." Wyn situated himself on the couch.

"Is there drama at the Quick Lube? Or drama with Trish, perhaps?"

Wyn smiled, and revealed, "No drama."

"Well, then she's a keeper, an available blonde with no drama. What more could a guy want?" I sassed. His smile slowly faded.

"What is it with the wolf man? What makes you want him?" Wyn prodded.

I thought about it a moment--Peter's face, his jade-green eyes and strong jaw, his strong, yet calm, persona. "Attraction . . . connection . . . an overall feeling," I was smiling.

"Do you love him? Do you really, really love who he is, or is it just the idea of him, a John Doe, a wolf biologist?"

"I don't know, Wyn. But how will I ever know, unless I go?"

Wyn pondered this, and lightly offered, "Take your bear spray."

At this moment I loved Wyn. I loved him for not undermining me and my choices. He was a true friend, and the only person who wasn't belittling

154

me. I unfolded a blanket on the couch, tossed it over both of us, and grabbed the remote to the TV. The black-and-white classic *The Apartment* was playing, and I rested my head on his shoulder. "Thank you, Wyn." I could barely keep my eyes open, and exhaustion consumed me. I quickly gave up, and closed my eyes.

Wyn put his arm around my shoulder and stringed his fingers through my hair. "I worry about you, Maggie."

"Well, don't." I muttered, still with my eyes closed.

"I do."

"Don't."

He laughed. "Okay, I won't." And that was my last memory before I fell asleep. I vaguely remember being put to bed, but the emotional exhaustion of the evening overcame me and I sank into the warm sheets with Wyn comforting me by his presence on the couch.

Chapter Twelve: Woods

The gray morning drizzle reminded me to add waterproof clothing to my backpack. I left a note for Wyn, who was passed out on my couch and making a funny slurping sound with each breath. I left him a note to stay in my loft while I was gone, and left a key.

Morning had not yet broken, but I was antsy to get on the road to meet Peter before his departure. He didn't exactly encourage me to join him, but he had not entirely discouraged it either. I munched on a breakfast bar, somehow pushing the sad reality of the robbery last night out of my mind, to embrace the hopeful spirit of the adventure before me.

I arrived in Wallace and parked the car in a back lot. I gathered my supplies, tossing the bear spray in one pocket, and checked my mirror to tousle my hair and apply a quick layer of lip gloss. I looked tired, but presentable. As I approached his front door, I could feel my heart palpitating. This was it. I was finally entering his life. I knocked lightly, not wanting to wake the neighbors. I knocked again, and amidst the second knock, the door opened three inches, until it slowly opened wide. Peter stood there, dressed in heavy camouflage pants and thick layers under his weatherproof shell. He neither smiled nor frowned, but just looked at me devoid of expression.

I looked right back at him. With all the thoughts and phrases I had practiced in the car, I only came up with the lame greeting: "Good morning," and smiled through my clenched teeth. After a long moment of staring, Peter stepped outside his apartment, and shut the door all but one inch. He said nothing. My heart was racing now. What if I couldn't come with him? What if he really meant no? It was a dance, the dance to be accepted or rejected. He had to take the lead, and I would follow. He stared at me intensely, until finally putting his arms around me, pulling me toward his chest in a big, comforting hug. He held me for a minute or two, resting his chin on the top of my head, and then his hands started to rub the back of my sweatshirt. As he pulled away, he said, "You are one persistent fool."

I nodded, "I'm going."

"There's no hotels, no running water, no amenities," Peter warned.

"I'm going." I smiled.

"You're going," he repeated in resignation. He shook his head, as in disbelief, but opened the door all the same. "Come in," he said, as he opened the door for me. "Don't be alarmed." On his bed and his table were two dart guns, multiple tranquilizers, a handgun, a box of bullets, a first-aid kit, and two packs of water, food and maps. He also had a bunch of computer equipment, radios, batteries, film, screwdrivers, ratchets, padlocks and keys. At the foot of his bed he had a full gas can and a double-bagged box of matches.

I took it all in, the adventure sitting before me. I was up for it. It would be my first time staying overnight in the woods, really roughing it. I was chomping at the bit to prove to Peter that I belonged with him, no matter what the geography. He started loading gear into his pack, which resembled one of those oversized army duffle bags with a harness. I had my backpack, which now looked school girlish in its dainty size. Peter was silent while he sorted and wrapped t-shirts around technical equipment. I saw a few food items, such as a jar of peanut butter and dehydrated fruit, instant coffee and beef jerky.

Peter finally broke the silence. "How's the kid?" He didn't stop packing or look up.

"Donny? He bolted. I don't even think he knows he got tranquilized." At this I couldn't help but laugh, just the sound of it.

Peter looked up at me, not amused. "I can't lose my job."

"You won't. I made sure of that. You protected me and my future. Dad understands that."

"Does he understand you coming out here, to the woods, with a stranger?"

"He knows. Look, it doesn't matter what my parents think. What matters is what I think. Peter, I am nineteen. I'm young, I know. But I see the way you look at me--" I stopped ranting, because I didn't want to chase him away. After a moment, I asked in earnest, "If you don't want me to come, I won't."

Peter continued packing and zipped up his pack. When he was done, he admitted, "I'd enjoy the company."

After loading his gear in his car, we drove in silence as the sun was peeking over the horizon. We drove east on Interstate 90 for thirty minutes and exited at Lookout Pass, a popular ski resort on the Idaho-Montana border. We drove past the parking overflow and entered a small neck of woods, where we parked the car at a trail head.

The silence between us was natural. Somehow this journey felt sacred, and too much chatter would complicate the simplicity of my enjoyment of being with Peter. Upon the first step out of the car, the brisk cold whipped down my spine and I knew I had to get my parka on quickly, along with a winter hat and mittens. I reached into the car and grabbed my wallet and cell phone, to zip into the outer pocket of my backpack. My phone was beeping--a missed message. I opened it to see the warning of low battery, and then it indicated power failure.

"No sense bringing those things," Peter commented. "Where we're going, there's no service of any kind."

I tossed my phone into the glove compartment, along with my wallet. I tugged at my backpack, stretching it around my layers. Peter helped me reach the loop that was evading me. He was loading his own self with a huge pack and I, in turn, helped him fit it to himself.

"Where to?" I asked, after he locked his car after placing a National Forest Service Permit in his windshield.

"We hike three miles to site 7." Peter must have seen the look on my face. I wasn't expecting to feel so out of place, so cold and disoriented in the thick woods. "We may have to do a little trailblazing. You can handle three miles, right?"

"I can handle three miles in my running shoes," I answered, although I wasn't exactly feeling confident.

It was a dense wood, not your ideal for hiking, obviously not a thoroughfare for outdoor enthusiasts. The trail made a quick ascent, and although I was thrilled to be with Peter, my shortness of breath did not allow for any talking. One hour later, we reached a clearing where we dropped our packs. A blood-orange sunrise greeted us, and Peter pointed at it. "Have you ever seen anything so raw?" Peter's mood was relaxing. He was comfortable here. He took out two water bottles and we sat on a log and stared at the morning sky.

After rehydrating, Peter took out a log book and noted that the last date of this visit was on August 12. He walked to a wooden box in the middle of the clearing, which was locked with a padlock, and keyed into it. He opened the lid to find a plastic-covered camera set up to a timer. He picked up the camera, which was powered off, and removed the chip from inside. "The camera has a fifteen-day life span, so the info is old, from August. Let's see what we got." He took out his laptop and inserted the chip. Footage of the meadow rolled on and on, an occasional chipmunk hopping across the summer meadow, mimicking a scene from Bambi. White-tailed deer grazed in the meadow, wandering in and out. Peter put the video on fast-forward and it flickered through uneventfully.

"What do you do with the footage?" I questioned. Watching the footage seemed exciting until nothing happened.

"I'm hoping for an appearance by the wolves. The Clearwater pack has a fifty-mile range as far as I know, and is the closest to civilization. At last count, there were eight of them. They circulate their territory about every ten days or so. Hopefully, they'll make an appearance."

"Is that why you're studying them, to police them?"

"To research them. We have state counters who gather wolf numbers for each region. I'm more focused on one particular pack, and their resilience.

Peter glanced at the laptop, which was still forwarding the days, with lack of motion. "Conservationists claim that wolves maintain balance in the ecosystem. Wolves provide food for other scavenger animals, and they are selective killers, weeding out the weak in a herd, and ultimately strengthening the elk and deer prey as a whole. Conservationists want them protected by the feds under the Endangered Species Act. They feel hunting the wolves threatens their existence. They want the wolf hunt stopped. "

"We shouldn't hunt wolves, anyways." I said. It was obvious to me that wolves were part of nature, and were useful. "Humans don't eat wolf meat, so there's no benefit to us, other than plain sport."

Peter's jade eyes looked right into me, reflecting on what I'd just declared. Then he continued, "There's always a flip side to every controversy. Wolves eat a lot. They kill a lot. Mostly it's in the wild, but occasionally it's cattle. Ranchers aren't too happy about their cattle being threatened, and hunters aren't happy about their predation decreasing the elk populations. Controlled hunting can stabilize the wolves' rapid population growth and minimize their dominance. Subsequently, wolves have been delisted, and re-listed, and delisted again. Some hunters want to get rid of the wolf, period. Some want to hunt for the sake of getting a wolf, some want to hunt to protect their livelihood, and environmentalists want to protect the wolf, period. Hunters argue the wolves are thriving. Conservationists argue that there is no solid management plan to ensure the wolves don't become overhunted and, eventually, eliminated again. They plea to the feds, through the courts, to relist the wolves on the Endangered Species Act, to force an end to legalized wolf hunts. The issue is very real, and lawsuits are endless between the parties.

"What do you think?" I asked Peter. "You must have an opinion, because you're out here, seeing the data."

"I can't have an opinion. I have to be unbiased and present the research. Any bias, and I could compromise the validity of the data, and my job."

"The states want to allow hunting because it stabilizes the wolf population and brings in so much money, and the feds want to ensure the wolves are protected." I was seeing the dilemma.

"That's right."

"So whom do you work for, the state or the feds?"

"Idaho Fish and Game contributes to my salary, and the feds match it. I work for both, to provide unbiased, current research to both parties to use in lawsuits, lawmaking, anything. And I must stay incognito. This is a battle of wills, a very heated battle."

"Do you feel threatened?" I asked. It was becoming clear why nobody knew about his accident.

"Undercover is best. They leave me alone, to do the research, to live in the field at times, and gather the data that will hopefully stand solid for

162

both parties. I send in reports when I get what I need."

"Can you prove sustainability?" I asked. "You're just studying one pack."

"I'm trying. I've got some systems in place, or did, before the accident, that were making real measurable strides in determining if hunting will overall hinder the survival of a pack. I knew of two packs in this region, and have studied both. I collared most of them and was able to follow-up on them. Right now, hunters can buy a wolf tag, and the states set a limit to how many wolves can be harvested. The problem for sustainability is a hunter has no idea if they are shooting a yearling, a beta or the alphas--male or female. Such kills can be devastating to the entire pack."

"The whole pack dies if the alphas are shot?"

"That's one thing I'm trying to measure. So far, the wolves are reproducing at a healthy, if not vigorous, rate, resulting in more wolf tags being allotted. What impact all the harvesting has on their stabilization is what I'm trying to determine."

"Through counting?"

"Yes, primarily."

"So that's it. You track, collar, and count wolves."

"By land and air--this one specific pack--while observing their behaviors."

"It's fascinating. It's such a gray area, whether to allow hunting of a pack animal that we've tried so hard to reintroduce here." I felt inspired, and in awe of the fact that Peter was undercover here, embracing isolation for the importance of the work.

"Some people absolutely hate these wolves, and some love them with their lives," Peter admitted.

Suddenly, the screen flickered with some jolting, and then an animal came quickly into view. Peter jumped to the screen, slowed it down to real time, to see a gray wolf walk in front of the camera, approach the box, and stick its nose right in the front. The beautiful canine was curious, trying to perceive the foreign object in the bounds of his or her territory. After sticking its nose on the box, it nudged the box several times, causing the camera to wobble. Then it gave up. Peter rewound the footage and watched it again. He rewound it again, logged the date and time on the camera, and then stopped the footage. Using the zoom function, he scoped into the woods. There was gray fur, totally camouflaged, in the woods. He rewound. For two hours of logged time, the wolf stared down the box, observing, learning and studying the box before approaching it. Peter zoomed left, then right. Two more furry creatures sat, watching. Then the one approached the box, as he had studied several times.

"That's the alpha?" I asked, feeling smart that I knew a few things about wolves, thanks to Jack London's *Call of the Wild* and *White Fang.*

"Yep. Number 24."

"Why not name him?" I teased. "Like Buck, or Firestorm, or something other than 24."

"Unbiased. Naming them is too personal. I've got to prove an unbiased study."

"You can't possibly be unbiased. Look at him. He's beautiful. He's powerful and a leader. Shooting him would mean the other two in the woods would struggle to survive."

164

"I'm hired to provide evidence, not give my biases."

"Well, you're wise then, protecting your heart."

"Fulfilling my contract. I'm not paid for my opinion, but my data."

"Well, I'd name him . . . Bob."

Peter laughed. "The alpha, Bob?"

"Bob. If you have to stay emotionally neutral, I'd name him Bob. But, if you could believe in him—believe in his leadership and power—I'd name him Ryker. Ryker has strength and power. Ryker, the alpha male.

"You think a lot," Peter said.

"Let me get this straight: You are employed by Idaho Fish and Game along with a federal grant to track wolves, collar them, and get a seasonal count. Then they use your data to either justify or adjust the state wolf-management plan for hunting and protecting." I was excited that I could believe in his work, and his work was so vital.

"And I'm on call to be available for hearings."

"Hearings, like as a witness in court?"

"Sometimes I have to make an appearance at public hearings as an expert specialist, sometimes on the witness stand, and sometimes for depositions." Peter chuckled to himself. "So those are the times I'm pulled off the mountain, to send in my reports and deal with a lot of angry people. I prefer it up here."

"Are they thriving?" I asked. "Are the wolves thriving, like they say?"

"So far. Anything could change." Peter was done screening through the video and logging the IDs of the wolves into his notebook. "Alpha male with two yearling sons. I just wish I knew where the rest of the pack was. I've lost a bit of time in hotel Kootenai Medical." He shut his laptop and put it in his pack. "You ready for site 8?"

I studied him. He was different here. He wasn't calloused, cold, or resentful. He was free; his spirit was at home. I felt completely foreign, and it was exciting. Never in my life had I been in an unmarked territory, totally in the wild, with wolves hiding in the shadows. It was thrilling, scary, and unknown.

"Are you ready?" he said again, breaking me out of my daydream. "You okay?" He looked worried.

"I'm more than okay." I smiled, and he grabbed my hand and led me through the forest where the wolves on video had just been hiding.

"Good, because this is where it gets fun." We hiked into the woods ten minutes and found what appeared to be a poorly-constructed stone shack, padlocked in front with double doors. On the front was a plate stating *Federal Property, Keep Out.* Peter pulled out a key on his keychain and unlocked the door. Inside was a Yamaha 450 dirt bike. I looked at him, wondering why a perfectly incredible motocross bike was locked up in the woods. I knew a tiny bit about motocross as Donny had ridden in the county fairs as a kid and liked to ride in the woods. This bike was out of his league. Peter was fondling the bike as if it were a long lost pet that needed grooming. "I never told you about the other woman in my life," he teased. He found a rag in the shack and dusted her off. Then he grabbed a sleek black helmet, "Ready to ride?"

Chapter Thirteen: Cave

Peter put the helmet onto my head and buckled it under my chin. "Site 8 is twenty-two miles down the road. We ride." He grabbed the handlebars and rolled the bike out of the shack. Then he locked the shack, before securing his equipment onto the bike with bungee chords. He nestled an extra pack onto the front of his chest. "Hop on, and hold tight. This is going to be a bumpy ride."

"You need a helmet," I pointed out. "You just got your head put back together."

He had uncapped the gas, checking the levels. "There's only one." He was determined. I didn't feel comfortable pushing it. He quickly checked the oil, the water, and then declared, "Having second thoughts?" He was toying with me, but it was welcomed. I thrust my leg over the bike, and he jumped on quickly in front of me, and kicked down to start the engine. I wrapped my hands around his waist. We raced off through the woods on an unmarked trail that he seemed to know well. As we rode, I imagined what a life with Peter would be like. I couldn't imagine him being here alone anymore. I planned in my mind to never allow that to happen again. I could envision partnering in his research, studying the wolves, living in nature, not having to tolerate the social expectations of city life anymore. The more I thought about it, the more it seemed like the absolute perfect place for me. I loved being alone. I adored my loft, mostly because it was so private, so alone. I'd miss my parents, but they were just a day-trip away. This could be so perfect.

My daydream was interrupted by a bumpy encounter with deep-rooted, washed-out trail, the bike gyrating and jostling us both. Peter slowed down and leaned back to yell, "Hang on tight!" and then he gunned it over some thicker roots. We got through the washout, and the ride settled down a bit. "You still hanging on?" he yelled, and I nodded, not wanting to admit that my rear was sore and my arms were aching. I was not going to whine, not now that I had him convinced that I was strong.

We arrived at site 8 an hour and a half later, which revealed a big clearing where you could see down into the wetlands and a river at the base. Again, Peter had a wooden locked box housing what I assumed was his second camera. He parked the bike just out of the woods, and massaged my neck a bit, asking if I managed the bumpy ride. I told him I was fine, just maybe a bit hungry. He was eager; he was excited; he was a different man; and I loved his little-boy enthusiasm that lit up his face. He rummaged through his pack, digging for snacks. While he was searching, I noticed him stumble and drop to one knee, unnaturally. "Peter?" I asked.

Peter braced himself on the large pack, and took a few breaths. "I think I'm hungry too. Did we skip breakfast?"

"We did." The morning was such a rush, from the moment I knocked on his door, to his

168

acceptance of me, to this wild chase through the woods. It must be around three o'clock.

Peter pulled out a box of soda crackers and some dehydrated beef jerky. I would have given anything for a scone and a glass of orange juice. I sipped on a water bottle and tried to wash the unappealing snack down. I then remembered I brought granola bars and dug those out of my pack. Peter sat next to me, staring at the clearing. Then he began to talk. The thrill was a slow buildup in his voice, the excitement of his purpose. "This is hunting grounds, one of many, but one that I hope to get some footage of. Elk, deer, even moose will graze here, near the river. The wolves will pick one victim and pursue it until they fail as a group or succeed with a kill." He scanned the valley introspectively. "Come on, I want to show you something." Peter grabbed my hand and we walked through the clearing. He was scanning the grassy area, looking, searching for clues to something I wasn't yet privy to. We came across what appeared to be rib bones of a large ungulate, or hoofed animal, with a few smaller bones nearby, and a large femur bone only steps away. "They've made a kill. I'll be a happy man if I have it on tape." We continued to walk down by the river, looking for tracks. I didn't notice anything, and yet Peter was surveying every inch of the land. "They haven't been here in a while."

"How do you know that?" I asked.

"The bones are completely clean; they've been scavenged. When the wolves are satiated, they move on and leave the leftovers for coyotes, eagles, crows. I don't see any tracks, any scat, nothing that they would have left to mark with. They'll be back. They come back to remark about every nine or ten days."

"Will we see them?"

"It's unlikely. Most men will never see a wolf in the wild. They are evasive creatures. But if we get out of their way, it's possible, if we stay long enough."

I wasn't prepared to watch a live pack attack. I had video footage more in mind. "How long are you planning on staying?"

"Until I get what I need. Or supplies run out."

"Or the weather gets too cold?" I added. It was nearly December, and dry. Around here four feet of snow is not uncommon without a moment's notice in these parts.

"Weather won't be a factor. Wolves love the winter. This is their season to shine, and the best season to get research evidence." Peter looked at me, still with the introspection that I couldn't figure out. His lips finally pursed a smile, and he grabbed my hand. "Are you okay, Margaret? Tell me what's going on in your head."

"I'm okay. I'm more than okay," I assured him. "I'm sort of in awe, really."

"I didn't think you would make it this far." He admitted. "What do you say, can you hang around here with me for a day or two?"

I was so alive with Peter that the cold air and the hunger pangs in my stomach seemed inconsequential compared to the sheer thrill of being with him. "I can rough it."

Peter held my hand and led me back to where we arrived, where he had parked the motorbike. There was a group of boulders, quite large, one in particular jetting tall, creating a concave area that could offer shelter from wind and rain. He faced me toward them. "Do you see it?" He was smiling, nervous excitement in his face. I had no idea what I was looking for. "This is where we will be *roughing it*." He looked straight toward the mossy boulders, satisfied.

"You brought a tent, right?" I was hoping that he wasn't assuming that the small underhang of the boulder would actually replace the need for a tent.

"I have something a little cozier in mind." Peter was trying to resist revealing his huge grin, like it was Christmas morning or something.

I looked at him, confused. He led me to the boulder, and I stood looking at it, and then upon closer inspection, saw a three-foot gap behind the obvious shelter. The rock had cracked and left a gaping entrance to what Peter was encouraging me to explore. Peter lifted a six-foot log that he had nestled in front of the crack, opening up an entrance into a hidden cave. I hesitantly walked into the rock cave, and streams of natural light shone through two openings in the roof of the twelve-by-twenty-foot cave. It was beautiful, natural, and what took my breath away is that it was furnished like a tiny little apartment.

"What is this?" I asked, barely audible through the wonderment I was feeling. Peter said nothing, but was intent on watching every expression I made.

There was an enchanting wooden table with several candles on it, two chairs, a platform bed made of chiseled wood just a foot off the ground with eggcrate padding for a mattress, sheets, a bedspread and pillow. On one wall was a bookshelf, half filled with food all in plastic bags, and the other with books, magazines, playing cards, and a photo of Peter and a woman. In the far corner the cave was bare, with nothing nearby but scorch marks along the wall, some large rocks creating a fire pit, and some fire utensils including a grid, a poker, a hand axe, and a small shovel. There was even a fire extinguisher nearby the stack of chopped and stacked wood. Peter felt the bedsheets which were cold and moist. "A bit damp, I'm afraid. They need a little drying out."

"You live here." It was more of a proclamation than a question. "You make a fire over here, and live in this cave?"

"I do. How's this for roughing it?" He was proud of himself.

It dawned on me that I wasn't going to have to eat crackers and beef jerky for days. He had an entire stock of shelf food, from dried milk, to beans, canned fruit, soup stock, biscuit mix, enough to actually eat well. The joy suddenly dissipated to curiosity and confusion as I thought I had finally grasped what Peter was doing as a field biologist. He had an apartment in Wallace. The state pays all his bills, only to expect a number count every three months. Other than that, they left him alone.

"Fish and Game doesn't know about this place, do they?" I asked him.

"Only one person knows about this." He looked at the photo of the woman.

"Who is she?" I asked, realizing that Peter had a past before me, a relationship, maybe current, that I never even considered. How did I forget to ask him all these questions? Everything seemed in the cards for us, but I may have given fate too much trust.

172

Peter looked pained when he spoke her name, "Maya. She's just a very bad memory for me. But she's gone." He took the photo and placed it facedown.

The cave had the charm of a gingerbread house. Maya must have had a hand in that, I guessed, after seeing the disaster of his apartment in Wallace. I was starting to feel completely vulnerable to my naiveté and wondered where Maya was. Why was she not with Peter? What had happened between them? Did Peter do something to her? This was starting to feel like a very bad dream. I quickly stepped outside the cave and took a few calming breaths. I walked toward the motorbike, picked up my pack, and stood still, angry.

Peter came after me slowly, cautiously. "What's wrong?" He was gentle, confused, hurt. "I thought you would like this."

"Please take me home." My back was turned. I couldn't face him.

"What's wrong?"

"You live in a cave. You track wolves. Your girlfriend is missing although you still have her picture. Nobody knows where you are. Nobody knew you in the hospital. Nobody knows you now." I pinched my eyes shut, hoping that would prevent any tears from escaping. My hands were shaking and I shoved them in my pockets. I felt like such a fool, to trust a man I didn't know, a man I pursued when he was helpless.

"Don't." Peter was firm. "I can take you home right now, and if you want me to, I will. But I am not the crazy man in the woods."

"Who are you then? And where's Maya?"

Peter looked at me, staring in disbelief, and then rolled his eyes up to the sky. "Oh, god. I can only imagine how this looks." Peter kicked the ground and then started to nervously laugh. "I am Peter Delano, and everything I've told you is true. I haven't told you everything though." Peter laughed again, only making me more scared. "I've told you the facts, because that is how I operate. Here's the emotions: I love my job--I love it too much. I want to be here all the time and, unfortunately, Maya didn't want to be alone so much in the city. I tried to make it comfortable for her here. She fixed it up a bit, but it still wasn't her. I thought she was the one. The one I would never regret. She found someone else, and left. That was three years ago."

I turned to him, and he was staring at me. "I knew this was a mistake, showing you the cave. I'll take you home."

I looked at Peter, the heartache revealed in his eyes. "I've never seen anything like this." Then I walked toward him, now realizing that I believed him, that everything he was telling me was the truth. "Why this extreme?"

"I don't know. I don't know what causes people to go to extremes." He gave me a glance, sort of a touché. "Do you?"

I knew in that moment that Peter understood why I crossed the line, why I lied about being his fiancé. "A connection."

Peter nodded, and repeated, "A connection." He smiled at me, and then reached for his pack and swung it around his shoulder. "It'll be dark soon. Hop on." Peter grabbed the helmet off the motorcycle.

"Wait," I said. "How about we start over?"

"Start over?"

174

"Let's start over. Before we go one more mile together, let's just introduce ourselves, the right way."

"Is that what you need?" he asked.

"I need to know the whole you, hidden caves and all. No more surprises."

"All right, fair enough." He held out his hand to introduce himself. "I'm Peter, thirty-two-year-old field biologist with Idaho Fish and Game. I live most of the time in a cave out in the Clearwater Wilderness, but I return to Wallace for periodic stays to send in reports to the state and to present the research. I enjoy anything to do with nature, and apparently have been known to hibernate only to awake engaged to a beautiful girl half my age." I rolled my eyes and received his hand, and he shook it. He paused for a moment, and then added one interesting detail. "There's one more thing. I am researching something on my own. I'm hoping to prove something about the wolves' nature, something that hasn't been proven before, not with solid research. That's my last secret. That's what makes me stay here, live here."

Peter has an alternative agenda. He was on the brink of breakthrough research. "Are you going to let me in on the covert operation?"

"In time, if you feel you can handle it." He was being sassy, which helped with my return introduction.

"First of all, girls mature much faster than boys, so the age thing isn't really that big of a deal, if you don't make it. I'm Margaret, nineteen-year-old jewelry designer at Whitaker Jewelry, and I live in a loft above the store--my own cave of sorts. I live and breathe in the family jewelry shop and have since I can remember. I enjoy running and reading, and get carried away with the illusion of fate, which has caused me to delude myself to think I can save people. I plan to take over Whitaker Jewelry one day soon."

Peter looked at me thoughtfully, and then shook my hand, holding it still with both his hands. "Okay, let's go, before it gets dark."

"I want to stay," I assured him. "I want to see the wolves." I smiled at him, hoping he would realize that I was open to becoming part of his life, possibly the way Maya wasn't.

"You want to stay? Here?"

"Yes, I want to stay here, with you." There was tension between us, a moment where again, Peter had to hear what I was saying and believe me. "I trust you."

Peter was lost in thought, until he finally put the helmet back on the bike and tossed his pack down. He looked at me with a smile and declared, "The footage. I need to get the footage." He took me by the hand, and we raced to the locked box, where Peter took out his keys and unlocked it. Again, there was a similar camera, shut down and out of battery life. "You really want to stay?" he asked again, with joyous relief on his face.

I assured him, "I want to know everything. It's crazy, I'll admit. But it's amazing too. The wolves are amazing. Your work is amazing." I looked at the simple video camera that he was holding. "Don't you have a better way of tracking them," I asked, "a more accurate device to track where they are right now? Isn't that what their radio collars are for?"

"I do have an antenna in the shed back at the base that I can use. And I do use it, but mostly for when I fly. I'm hoping to find something on tape that I can't find just through radio signals." He put the disc into his laptop, and we scanned through video footage on fast-forward, like before. Herds of white-tailed deer were grazing near the riverbank. "This is good. This is what they will feed on. This is their prey. Where is the predator?" The tape went on, and night fell, and the deer continued on and dispersed. The footage continued, and continued. No wolves appeared. The disc suddenly ran out, as battery life gave way on his laptop. "Nothing."

"So far, you've only got record of the alpha male and two yearlings. How are you going to account for the rest of the pack?"

"By air, if I have to. I can use that radio antenna and charter a helicopter to locate and count them. I try not to, as our funds are limited; I can only rely on that occasionally."

I grabbed his log book and flipped back to the last entry before his accident. "You have here a pack of eight, with an alpha male and female, three yearlings, and three mature betas. We saw the alpha and two yearlings already. If not by air, what is the plan to track--"

"Ssshhhh," Peter held his hand in front of my face. He had binoculars at his eyes, aimed across the river about a quarter of a mile away. He was whispering now. "I count seven." I didn't know what he was talking about, as I didn't see anything. He quickly handed me the binoculars. "Here. Hold these while I grab the camera. Just don't move." I took the binoculars and looked. In the far distance, just emerging from the opposite woods, across the river, were the wolves. I heard the telescopic camera snap, snap, snap. Peter was shooting stills, close-ups of every wolf. He was whispering to himself, "Come on, turn your head."

He snapped more pictures. "Seven. Seven wolves. One's gone. Either deceased, or possibly a yearling left the pack to find a mate. Those are good numbers."

I was amazed, watching these animals as they romped through the grassland, and then disappeared back into the woods. "They're gone." I whispered to Peter. "Did you get what you needed?"

"They're not gone. They are near. And they must not know we are here, or they will stay away. As for a count, yes, I got what I needed for the state. But they're preparing to hunt. They're marking their territory, but also sensing the prey's location." Peter dug through his pack quickly and put another disc in the video camera, replaced the battery pack, and stuck it back into the wooden box. "I'm hoping to record the hunt."

"So we wait?"

"We wait." He had finished loading the camera lockbox, and was smiling as he looked at me. "Out of sight--in the cave."

His charm couldn't be beat. I was ready to put the wolves aside and hunker down in the cave. Who knew where the night would lead. I was not wanting to rush anything, yet totally willing to rush everything. Like nature. What happened next, I did not expect.

Chapter Fourteen: Wolves

Peter dropped to his knees, and I thought he was funny, until his upper body joined his base on the floor. Peter was seizing. His mouth was open, his tongue was out, and his body twitched in frightening, shivering convulsions.

"Peter?" I said to myself for that one second where I was convinced he was joking. "Ohmygod, Peter!" Yelling for help wasn't going to do anything. What are you supposed to do for seizures? I remembered a girl in my high school class had a seizure in line at the cafeteria. The lunch attendant backed everyone away and rolled her on her side and just held her. I dropped to my knees and rolled Peter to his side and held his head safe. It seemed like an eternity, but it most likely lasted about twenty seconds. Peter was bleeding on his forehead where he had hit the ground, and there was blood on his teeth. His eyes fluttered open, but he didn't try to say anything. He looked exhausted. I stroked his hair and told him to relax, that everything was fine.

We sat in the field for ten minutes after his seizure, until I helped Peter stand up. I supported his waist and we walked gently back to the cave. Peter did not bring any of his medication with him, and I was determined that we needed to get back to town in case something worse were to happen.

Peter didn't argue with me, but told me that we would have to leave in the morning, as it was nearly dark. I was suspicious if the jostling motorbike ride had been too intense for him. He had only been out of the hospital about a month. What was he thinking? What was I thinking, allowing him to do this? Peter was the kind of guy you just didn't tell what to do.

I walked him into the cave and lit the candles. I made Peter lie down, and he didn't argue. I think the entire episode scared him and wiped him out. Within moments, he was sound asleep. The candles were beautiful, but the cave was overall damp and cold. I took a candle outside and gathered a few small twigs and grasses to start a fire with. Inside, I found a plastic bag with a box of matches. "Thank you, Peter," I whispered to myself, knowing I'd never rub sticks hard enough to gather a spark. I lit the grass and twigs, and it caught fire easily. I added more and more twigs, until the twigs produced substantial flames. I then took one piece of wood from the pile and chopped it into small pieces of kindling. The fire was roaring and warm, and the smoke filtered up through the hole in the cracked ceiling above.

I rummaged through his bookshelf of bagged food and found some Pop-Tarts and dehydrated apples and apricots. I sat at the table with the finger food and ate to the sound of plangent howling. The wolves were back. I listened to them call, the mournful cry beckoning their family to gather near. Their sound wasn't close, but could be heard reverberating through the valley. Peter would want me to wake him, but I knew he was in a deep rest. I considered using his binoculars to scope the wolves' position, but I was afraid they

180

would see me. As much as my book knowledge told me the wolves wouldn't hurt me, just being this close gave me cause to fear them. I stayed in the cave, stoked the fire, and counted the minutes turn into hours as the night passed. I sat next to the fire all night, stoking it and waiting for dawn to break. As the wolves howled through the night, something in me yearned for home. Donny was in trouble, Dad and Mom were scared, and Wyn was displaced at my loft. Nothing was normal right now. Nothing seemed safe.

Peter jolted in the bed, another seizure encroaching on his body. I rushed to his side, to see him tormented by the current of electricity misfiring from his brain. I now realized that the sudden commencement of seizures was due to the lack of medicine that his body was used to. His postcoma body wasn't ready to be independent from the drugs that help stabilize his brain waves. He needed help, and quick. The next jolt was quite violent, and I rushed to him to hold him still. His eyes were back in his head, and he was sweating bullets. I tore the blanket off him, and created a barrier for him to thrash against. While rearranging the blankets, a hard metal object flew to the ground. A cell phone. I stared at it incredulously. Peter was adamant that he hated cell phones, that they were an intrusion on life.

I powered it on, and Maya's picture appeared. The backlight flickered, searching for service. The battery life bar quickly went from five to four bars, before a "No Service Available" signal flashed. I looked up at the rock ceiling, and realized that I must try outside. With a candle in one hand, I took Peter's phone and walked steadily outside, away from the cave. Powering the phone on, the battery bar again dropped, now to three bars. "Roaming" flashed, and flashed, and flashed. I must be getting a signal from Interstate 90 somewhere along Mullan. The power bar slipped to two bars. Without wasting time, I texted Wyn: *U awake? Need help. St 8 Clearwater. Call me.*

I pushed send, and saw the message sent, just before one remaining bar of battery life flashed. The phone rang. Faithful Wyn was up, thank God.

"I've got to make this quick." I answered the phone.

"Are you hurt?" Wyn inquired, hostile.

"No, I'm fine. It's Peter. Wyn, he's not waking up. He's had two seizures, and he's not waking up."

The phone was silent. Then he whispered, "Call 911."

I couldn't do it. I couldn't call 911 after all I've done to deceive the hospital. I knew there were other options. "All I need is his medicine," I pleaded.

"It's not about you!"

"Wyn, please listen."

"What do you want me to do?" He was yelling.

"Find me! I don't know where I am, and Peter needs his medication. He's having seizures, and they're getting more frequent."

Wyn didn't respond. He was silent, and suddenly I realized why. The phone had died. I tried to power it back on, and it didn't have enough juice to even start up again. "I hate phones!" I threw the phone against the hard ground and watched it break in two.

Back in the cave, Peter slept while small seizures overtook his body randomly. I had cleared everything around him, and knew there was nothing else I could do but get him to his medicine. I couldn't just sit here and watch him like this. I had to take matters into my own hands.

I have never ridden a motorcycle on my own but was determined to get help. I rummaged through his backpack and found his keys. I went to Peter, and although I was pretty sure he couldn't hear me, I bent down and whispered in his ear, "Hold tight, Peter. I'm getting you help." I put the backpack around my shoulders and added a log to the fire before heading out of the cave.

The wolves had stopped howling, and I felt somewhat safer as I walked out into the blinding moonlight. The motorbike was under the natural shelter of the outer rock. I tried to visualize Peter starting the bike: turn the key, pull out the choke, and do a few other things which I never paid much attention to. The moonlight provided a bright light, which was helpful. I straddled the bike and familiarized myself with it. I saw a RUN/ON button, a fuel ON button, pulled the choke out, put the key in the ignition, and turned it to RUN. Then I depressed the throttle, and pushed the ON button. The engine started but died. Something's wrong, I thought. I tried it again with similar results. It was useless. I sat on the bike, and between myself and the moonlight, and possibly the God of this universe, I cried. I cried pathetic, angry, and raw. "Why?" I screamed. "Why can't ANYTHING just be easy for once?" I kicked the bike and then cursed at my toe. "Damn it!" I screamed at myself, now angry at my toe for having nerve endings. I hobbled around, crying pitiful sobs, and then suddenly came to a frozen halt.

I don't know how long he had been watching me. He was huge, gray with white patches. He was inquisitive and quite endearing, sitting on his haunches, his head cocked to one side, eyes wide open, ears perked up. As fate would have it, a gray wolf was studying me, the perplexing act of a human attacking a motorcycle. Our eyes locked in a stare and, under the blazing moonlight, we didn't move, neither one wanting to retract. I envied the wolf, who was merely twenty feet away, this dominant creature who lived among these hills, and who feared nothing. He was curious who trespassed in his territory, and no doubt was determining if he was going to accept or reject my intrusion. The wolf sat and stared. I slowly slid my hands into my coat pocket and stared right back. The wolf wagged its tail a bit, then did a playful leap in the air, and barked like a dog. He again sat on his haunches, resuming his glare. I stood stiff, unwavering in my stare, and gently but firmly pulled out my canister of bear spray, positioning my forefinger on the nozzle. I felt the draw of this god of the woods, beautiful and reverent and playful, and yet I knew his power. The wolf suddenly ran into the woods, disappearing like a ghost in the night.

I stood, finger still positioned on my only weapon, the bear spray. Numinous awe combined with fear encompassed me, an overwhelming sensation of sadness and regret combined with reverent beauty. The clearing smelled of purple, the minor key of sad holy music filling my mind, entrancing me. I stood face-to-face with a wolf, and now didn't want to go back in the cave. I wanted to follow that wolf into the woods and demand an explanation of his life, of what it was that Peter needed to capture on film to make his studies complete. Stop eluding him with your mysterious behavior, and show yourself, I wanted to insist. I walked into the field, past the camera box, and allowed the moonlight to guide me toward the stream. As I neared it, I realized there was a freshly- deceased white-tailed deer, medium in size, half floating in the water, half on shore. The hindquarters were torn apart, but the animal was intact. The neck was torn as well, most likely where the wolf tore through the jugular. A scampering and whipping of wings bolted out of the field beyond the stream, as a multitude of crows vanished in front of me. A huge bald eagle swooped in and landed in the field. I stood motionless as the majestic animal hovered over what I now realized was the site of kill number two, or what was left of it. The eagle had landed on the bloody carcass as it was nearly cleaned out, with the rib cage intact and a few pieces of ligaments and meat attached to some larger bones. The crows came back, challenging the eagle, and there was a tug-of-war for dominance on the carcass. The eagle flapped at the crows, talons threatening, never really committing to an attack, until it tore a long piece of flesh off and retreated into the air with its prize. The crows encompassed the kill again, safely.

It dawned on me that the deer carcass was about 50 yards in front of the camera box, and the remains of the second just yards further across the stream. Peter must have gotten the kills on film. If only he were awake to see what he had captured. I thought of Peter, and the camera box, and knew that the keys in the motorcycle also had keys to that box. I returned to the bike and retrieved the keys, and opened the lockbox. There, the camera was still rolling. I pushed stop on the machine and retrieved the disc, replacing it with a new disc in the machine. I was interfering with government research, but I knew that Peter was unable to retrieve it himself and would want to see what happened this very night.

I was curious too. What had these wolves been up to? I know that I could easily put the disc in his computer and find out, but his computer was government property. I went back to the cave, checked on Peter, who was still sleeping, and then rummaged through his backpack and found his notebooks and logs. I saw that he documented kill after kill, site, location, and animal. I knew he was tracking the wolves, but it seemed like he was tracking the victims as well. The date of kills seemed to be about five days apart, with one victim and about eight in the pack. Yet he had highlighted two kills on a single day back in the summer, with two victims. Why had he highlighted these? He made a note back in the spring from two years back: *Wolves kill what they need to survive: the weak, the young, or the sick. They restore balance in the ecosystem. Or do they? Does their predation wreak havoc instead of provide stabilization? ***What happens during a double kill?*

A double kill. What did that mean? This must be his research, his private research in addition to his wolf count. And he mentioned that he had been waiting to catch something on film, something that is additional proof. I reached for his laptop and turned it on, putting in the disc. A video program automatically opened, and I saw the disc icon ready to be played. I hit 'play' and watched as the footage immediately began with Peter's voice, "Out of sight. In the cave, if you're comfortable there." Then I heard a *thud* and myself shouting *Peter!* His seizure. The moment he had first seized was right after he changed the disc. I didn't want to relive it again.

I glanced at him, still asleep, but peaceful, and then found the fast-forward button. The field was still, dull, wavering a little from the footage. Then a herd of deer appeared on the screen, grazing in the twilight. I sat up and watched more closely as the herd, maybe twenty or so, drank from the river. Suddenly, tails shot up. All alert. I could see something in the woods. I pressed 'play' on the computer, and the footage slowed to real time. The glowing amber eyes in the woods revealed a wolf. I was so focused on following the blur of golden eyes that it startled me, this massive black beast as it chased a lone deer, nipping at her hindquarters. The deer kept running, in circles, nearly escaping, until another black and gray wolf cut her off and closed in from behind. They both gnawed at her until the deer stumbled. Suddenly the wolves from the pack joined, five more, and they took down the dominated deer. I nearly felt sick as I watched the wolves rip apart the deer, using their razor-sharp canines as butcher knives. They tear, rip, shred, feasting on the carcass. I had to fast-forward the cuisine, as it was raw and heartless. After a gluttonous meal, the pack sauntered away, but not too far, to lounge in the field, satiated after the kill. Again, I fast-forwarded the disc.

Suddenly, a single wolf stood up, stretched, and pranced a few paces toward the grazing herd of deer which, ironically, settled not too far from their enemies. In one huge alert, the herd bolted.

There pursued another chase, not even an hour after the first kill. One lone wolf singled out one juvenile deer. This small deer bolted across the screen, even jumping into the screen, as the single wolf clenched on its hindquarters, all caught on camera. The deer struggled to cross the river, the wolf hanging on. As the deer struggled out of the water, it stumbled with the weight and shock of a predator lock-jawed on its fanny. Seizing the moment of weakness, the wolf let go and sprang for her neck. Kill number two complete, the deer collapsed as if put into a trance, lying down slowly to her death. The wolf stood over his kill and began to howl. What shocked me most was after about five minutes of howling, it wagged its tail like any proud dog that caught a tennis ball, and sauntered off into the woods leaving the kill untouched. *This is what Peter wanted to capture. He got it on tape: A double kill.* I rewound the footage to examine the wolf again. The white and gray wolf wandered into the woods just outside of our cave. The very wolf I stared down moments ago.

I had just been face-to-face with a killer. I had an undeniable naiveté about the nature of these ferocious night-stalkers, and now I wanted to hide. The walls of the cave comforted me, but I knew that at sunrise I had no choice but to follow the motorcycle tracks on foot, running the twenty-two miles for help.

Peter started to tousle a little, opened his eyes, looked at me with uncertainty, winced as in pain, and shut his eyes again. I rushed to his side, stroked his hair, and watched him fall into a restful sleep. I wish that he could know about the footage, the double kill, and whatever it meant to his research. But his body was fighting some mix-up in signals that his brain refused to stop sending. The worry, the exhilaration of meeting the wolves, the fear of finding my way out was suddenly overcast by my own exhaustion. I stoked the fire, placed my backpack on the dirt floor, and lay next to the fire, propping my head on the pack as a pillow. My eyes became heavier and heavier, until I fell asleep in the dirt.

Chapter Fifteen: It is Real

I awoke to a pitchy shrill. I opened my eyes to see smoldering embers, the taste of dirt on my lips, and the cacophonic intrusion of my sleep repeating itself. I sat up, to hear Peter rustling, another small seizure overtaking him.

I rushed to Peter's side. "It's okay. I'm here. You're okay," I assured him, knowing this was anything but the truth. He wasn't okay, and I was no help. I watched as the spasms melted until they subsided, again. Shrills, now farther off, continued as syncopated rhythmic notes.

A whistle! A far off whistle! I ran out of the cave, the new day's sun shooting daggers of light at my eyes. In my haste, I didn't dare bother to brush the dirt from my clothing or out of my hair and face. I yelled, "I'm here! I'm here!" I ran into the clearing. "Anybody! Are you there?" I ran toward the woods, and then stopped short, remembering the gray wolf who owns this field. "Are you there? Please!" I pleaded. Another whistle, this time from the opposite direction of the cave, and then a four-wheeler shot through the meadow. The helmeted man rode up to me, stopped his ATV, pulled out a radio and announced, "I've got her. She's safe, at site 8." He then sat, staring at me, until he slowly pulled off his helmet.

"Wyn?" I cried, and nearly lost my balance as I ran toward him, not sure whether to trust what I was seeing.

Wyn was not alone. My father wheeled out of the woods behind him, with a forest ranger closely behind.

"Maggie!" my father shouted, and at that moment I became a little girl again, running to my father with overwhelming relief. He parked his ATV and stood, wrapping his arms around me as I let all strength dissipate.

"I'm sorry," I whispered, as he held me tight. "I'm sorry."

Dad put his hands on my face, and I whispered, "Peter needs help. He needs his medication." I led Wyn, the ranger and my father into the cave, giving minimal details to the ranger as fast as I could. Upon entering the cave and seeing Peter, the ranger immediately put on rubber gloves and injected Peter with a syringe. He then pulled out a radio. "Medivac to Clearwater, site 8 USFS; 46.5 latitude, -115.0 longitude. Head trauma, multiple seizures, victim known as Peter Delano with Idaho Fish and Game."

I brushed Peter's hair, as he breathed in and out steadily. Wyn looked around the cave in awe. Dad walked out, without saying a word. "How did you find me?" I asked Wyn.

"The Forest Service. They were able to reveal sites 7 and 8, for this emergency."

"My dad, he's probably so angry." I looked at Wyn, who couldn't look back at me.

"I can imagine." Wyn was looking at Peter, and I was suspicious that Wyn wasn't just referring to my dad.

"Is he going to be okay?" I asked the ranger. "I couldn't stop the seizures."

"I don't know," he said. "He had no business riding a bike this far out under those conditions." I didn't say a word, but accepted the rebuking personally.

"I better go talk to *him*." I told Wyn. He nodded, knowing exactly what I was in for.

I saw Dad, sitting on a boulder outside on the edge of the clearing. He looked to be entranced, the same way I was after meeting the wolf.

I walked to him, and he didn't acknowledge me. Was he praying? His eyes were wide open, and I knew that he was broken. I sat down next to him on the cold, wet rock. We sat, both staring at the field--words would be an intrusion to the conversation we were sharing. Dad didn't understand my deviation from the good child's life. Dawn was the one who had previously pulled these stunts. Knowing that I was the one to hurt him was painful.

"Love can do strange things to you, Maggie." Dad finally spoke. "It can pull you in directions that you are not meant for."

"Dad," I whispered. But it was pointless to defend myself. He had earned this lecture, and I was somehow yearning for it.

"Do you love this? This place? Being out here, secluded?"

I didn't know if it was a trick question, or if he was being sarcastic. "He does amazing work, Dad, important research."

"Do you love *this?*" he persisted.

"I love him."

"I've been nineteen, Margaret." There was pain in Dad's distant stare. "I've been nineteen, and in

192

love. I remember nineteen; I remember those feelings."

I realized that Dad was not trying to patronize my love for Peter, but trying against his usual wordless nature to communicate his life story. The silence of this place, Dad's silence, was screaming at me sudden truths that I didn't want to hear. "I've been nineteen before, and it is real."

In the silence following, sitting on the rock with my father, I cried. I cried for Dawn, my older sister, whose mother ran away when she was two years old. I cried for Donny, her little boy who was literally killing himself in addictions that were not filling his void. I cried for myself and for the adolescence that I finally revealed in myself, knowing that the shift to this adult life was not easy, emotionally. I thought I knew it all and now wondered why nineteen was so hard for me, for everybody.

The pulsating rhythm of the air ambulance was heard overhead, and over the horizon I could see the helicopter nearing. Dad surprised me and stood up, walked to the center of the field, and waved his hands in the air to alert the pilot. The pilot veered toward our field, and slowly descended, landing softly on the wet grass.

Wyn and the forest ranger appeared out of the cave, with Peter groggily leaning on their shoulders. I looked at him, not saying a word. He attempted to apologize to Dad and me, for the mess he made.

"No words, son. Not now," Dad said.

Peter looked at the video box, and tried to give directions to me, worried about his research.

"I'll take care of everything" I assured him. The helicopter was equipped with two EMTs who helped pull him in the side door. I saw them lay him down, and start an IV. He was going to be okay, I was assured. We all stood back, and the chopper lifted off.

The four of us watched him fly out of sight, and then stood in awkward silence.

"Let me go get his things," I announced at the three men who were staring at me.

I overheard the ranger say to Wyn aside, "Did you check out that cave?"

"Could be a job opening here," Wyn whispered back.

I shot Wyn a warning glare, until Dad interrupted, seeing me becoming heated. "Maggie, go get your things. It's time to go home." The way he said it was not a suggestion.

****

I rode Wyn's four-wheeler, and Wyn rode Peter's dirt bike that I was not able to start. The four of us, including Dad and the ranger, rode single file, the long twenty-two miles back to the stone shed, where I locked up Peter's bike. Now that Peter's work bike was secured, Wyn took back his four-wheeler, and I climbed on the back of Dad's ATV like a little girl clinging to her daddy. We drove the final three miles to the trail entrance to Peter's car. The forest ranger's vehicle and a trailer were parked alongside.

The ranger, whose name I never caught, took Dad back to Coeur d'Alene, and Dad insisted that Wyn drive me home in Peter's car.

As I got in the car with Wyn in the passenger seat, I felt his gaze dissecting me. "I don't need a psychologist, or a therapist, or a counselor." I was angry that nobody had seen the good in Peter, that

194

both Wyn and my father would allude to the creep factor.

"How about a driver?" Wyn looked at me carefully. "Could you use a driver?" Wyn asked.

"No," I snarled. But I knew how utterly exhausted I was and wondered if it showed on my face. "Yes, please." I scooted over to the passenger's seat, allowing Wyn to drive Peter's car. Wyn was a hero right now, loyal as sin, and truly caring. I made a mental note to ditch the annoyed persona and be nice. "Take the first exit into Wallace, and we'll pick up my car at Peter's place." Wyn remained silent, but I imagined he was shocked that I have been to Peter's residence. He started the car, and I quickly amended my request. "Actually, skip Wallace. I want to go straight to the hospital." Wyn remained cool, calm and silent. "I know I said it once before, but I want to thank you, for finding me, and for saving Peter."

Wyn glanced at the road ahead, finally offering a cool, "You're welcome." That was the last of our conversation, because unbeknownst to me, I faded off to sleep. I dreamed of the sun, of warmth, of the cozy blankets back at the loft, of my favorite spot on the couch, drinking warm cider and watching old cinema classics like *Roman Holiday*. I was with Peter, and he was working on a report on the other end of the couch. When I awoke, my dream wasn't too far off from reality, as I was in my bed, wrapped in my flannel sheets, the electric blanket on, radiating warmth to my tired and aching body. The only difference is I was alone. How did I get here? What time was it? By the time I finally dragged myself out of bed, I pulled the curtains to see it was dark. My alarm clock read 6 p.m.

I had slept all day. From the time we had returned to Peter's car at the trail head this morning, and with the hour-and-a-half drive home, I had slept half a day. How did I get up to my apartment? Why did I not wake up enough to refuse? I should be at the hospital with Peter. Wyn did this on purpose.

I heard music in the shop below, and upon descending, found Dad working behind the counter, adjusting a ring setting under a lamp. The shop was cleaned up, without a trace of the break-in two nights prior. Dad looked up at me and kept working, not wanting to lose focus. "Hey, Dad. It's past closing hours. Want me to lock up?" I asked, more as a formality than a true question. I slipped past him, and turned my key in the Sherman Avenue entrance.

"There's a new code for the new alarm. I've also got a new set of keys for the glass security release . . . that is, if you think you'll still be working here." Dad did not look up, focusing solely on steadying his pliers under the magnifying glass. "I always thought you would either go to college, or work with your old man. I never really considered a third option."

"I never considered a second option. It was always the shop, and working with you. I never planned . . ."

Mom came around the corner from the studio, polishing her own ring. "Mom." I walked to her and gave her a hug. "I'm sorry I worried you."

"Me? Worried?" Mom downplayed everything. "Concerned, yes. Worried? I wasn't worried . . . about you." Mom smiled the assuring, confident smile I've come to envy.

Dad was not resting for one moment from working on the setting, obviously avoiding me. I had truly disappointed him.

"I've always wanted to be here, Dad. I've never wanted anything else, until now." I paused, and Dad still didn't look up. "I'm going to go to the hospital. I can't be here without knowing how he is."

"He's been released," Dad muttered, finally dropping his pliers and putting down the jewelry.

"What? Where is he?" Suddenly, I was the one out of the loop.

"He called here to ask for his car. Mom and I drove his car over to the hospital." Dad looked at me with a stern fatherly glare that I was not familiar with.

"So that's it? You took his car to him? He's in Wallace?"

"He went home." Dad was not offering much, which meant that he had information that he was refusing to share.

"Dad, what did you do?"

"I didn't do anything. I did, however, have a nice chat with Peter. He's a very nice man, a man too old to be pursuing my teen-aged daughter."

"Dad! How could you? You, of all people, should understand."

"Margaret," Mom interrupted. "Dad and I are concerned, concerned that you are making choices that are neither safe nor wise."

"I am not you!" I was nearly shouting. "Because of Peter, I'm excited to wake up every day. I'm creative in this shop, inspired, and passionate about everything out in this great big world. You know me. You know that I've always been . . . different. You, of all people, should know that. This one person, Peter, came into my life, and I feel right. He makes me better. And I think I do the same for him. Yes, he's thirteen years older than me, and I know I'm young, but I can't give up on the one person who is right for me because of an age difference."

Mom and Dad sat, stunned. I hated arguing, but I was afraid that I was going to lose him if I didn't fight for him. "And one final thing, just to set the record straight: I pursued him. He had nothing to do with pursuing me, a *teen-ager*. I visited him, I sought out him. He was in the hospital while you were away, and I visited him while he was John Doe. I didn't intend to fall in love, but I did. We did."

Mom and Dad were shell-shocked. I had to say the next part quickly, or I would never be able to say it at all. "I'm going to Wallace; I'm going to see Peter; and I hope you can understand that you won't be first in my life forever." I walked out of the storefront, confident of my stance, only to find that when I rounded the corner to the back parking lot, my car was gone. My car was still in Wallace where I left it, at Peter's.

"Dang it!" I swore at myself. "Way to show 'em, Mags." Standing in the empty parking lot, I pulled out my cell phone and called Peter.

The phone rang several times before he picked it up.

"Peter!" I said, relieved to hear his voice, his sweet, coherent voice. "Hey, I want to come see you, but I left my car at your place."

"Yeah, I noticed. I just got home a bit ago."

"I hate to ask you to come get me, but could you?"

"M, I don't think I can," he said, groggily.

"My Dad said something, didn't he? Well, don't listen to him. He's just overly protective. He's got issues with control and somehow--"

"I just took my medication; I can't drive like this."

"Oh. Well, I'll come to you. I'll find a ride."

There was silence on the line. Finally, Peter confessed, "I don't know. I just don't know."

"Don't say that. You're just tired." I could feel myself becoming desperate.

"I've got so much work to do," Peter added.

"Well, I have to get your research video to you. You'll need your research, and you won't believe what you caught on tape. I'll bring it to you. I'll find a ride."

Again, he was silent. I'm sure he was tired, but his silence was creating doubt, insecurity in me that I did not want to acknowledge.

"Peter, I'll be over tonight. Okay?"

"Okay, M." He was groggy, that was for sure.

I hung up, nervous energy overtaking my body. I couldn't allow Mom and Dad to see me vulnerable like this. I had just told them off, for the first time in my life.

I dialed Julie. I hung up. She was too far away and busy with college. What was I thinking? The only other person I could think to ask was not my biggest fan at the moment, but I knew that he would drop anything for me. And if there was ever a time to use someone, it was now, when I had no other option. I dialed Wyn.

"Good morning," he said, musing as he knew I had slept the day away and it was now evening.

"Well, thanks to you, I need a ride to Wallace. You were supposed to take me to the hospital, not home. Peter would have given me a ride back to my car, but I'm stuck. I need a ride, Wyn."

"I can't. I've got a date."

"Wyn! This is important."

"I need to see Trish, to clear things up with her. She's not so fond of me always . . . helping you."

"Uugh," I shuddered. "Any word from Donny?" Donny definitely owed me a favor or two. I could probably sneak a ride out of him as long as he was sober.

"Don't." Wyn was serious.

"What choice are you leaving me?"

"Wait for the morning. I'll take you," Wyn insisted.

"I can't wait," I said, and then knowing that it was a low blow, I jabbed, "You don't love her. You're just biding time with her. And I love Peter, and there's a lot at stake. I wish you could just understand."

Wyn was silent. I know I hurt him, but it was true. I knew it and he knew it. His relationship with Trish was not what he wanted. Wyn wanted what I had with Peter, and I swore I would never be one to inject superiority over others, but no one was taking us seriously, and I was running out of options. "Call me in the morning if you still need a ride," was all he said, and he hung up.

I stood there, with my phone in my hand, about to call a cab, when Mom and Dad came around the corner.

"Mags?" Mom questioned. "I thought you were gone?"

I humbled myself to respond, "Well, my car is in Wallace. Minor detail I overlooked. I can't find a ride to get my car."

My parents looked at each other, and again I felt like the unprepared child with that judgmental scolding approaching. Mom finally said, "I'll take you to Wallace."

Then Dad offered, "I'll take her. You go home and enjoy the evening."

Mom insisted, "I need a little time with my daughter. I'll see you at home, Dear." Dad nodded, and walked home.

Driving with either of my parents to Wallace was the last thing I wanted to do, but I had no choice. It was that or pay $200 for a cab. I needed to see Peter and deliver his research to him safely. Mostly, I just needed to see him, to salvage any damage Dad may have caused. I got into Mom's car and sat silently. Mom was cheery and tried to make small talk, but I wasn't in the mood. I looked out the window, refusing to nibble on any bait.

"You know, your Dad told me he really liked Peter, thought he was decent enough." After I didn't respond, Mom persisted, "Your dad's scared. Don't you see that? You're a carbon copy of him-- smart, passionate, adventurous. He knows the fire of young love. He was married at nineteen."

"I've heard this so many times!" I said scathingly.

"Dad said that he could see Peter being good for you. You need someone who challenges you."

"He said that?"

"He did. As parents, you hope your kids grow up a bit, and then find love. Not the other way around. You are so much like your father, in every way. He knows what you'll do, because it's what he did."

I thought about that, how incredibly hard it would be to control something you love so dearly, to one day have to let it go. Suddenly, I felt ashamed of how I had reacted to my parents in the shop. "Sorry for what I said," I quietly admitted.

"You're nineteen. You can date whomever you choose."

"I was harsh. I was frustrated, because no one trusts my judgment."

Mom looked at me and then smiled. "I've always trusted you, Maggie. I still do." She was recollecting something, smiling through her thoughts. "I admire people who know what they want and go after it--in relationships, in careers. Knowing yourself is a huge gift. You know what you want and you go for it."

"I always thought I did, until I met Peter. He makes me willing to walk away from the shop and work with him, with the wolves."

Mom looked at me and smiled a knowing smile. "You have to decide if it's worth it."

"Do you have regret?" I asked Mom, seeing that look in her eye. "Dad didn't exactly propel your art dreams forward." Mom drove while silently reflecting as she stared out the front windshield. "I'm sorry. That's personal," I covered.

"You can ask me anything," Mom replied, as she prepared her answer. "I don't regret marrying your Dad. We have you."

This was the easy answer, and it covered the truth. "That's different. Without me, would you still marry Dad?"

Mom waited to respond, and I could tell she was formulating her response carefully. "I would not have done much with my art. I'm not entrepreneurial, like he is--like you are. I don't have that drive to succeed." Mom smiled, just thinking about her life with my father. "Your Dad is my partner in everything, and I don't just love him, I respect him. I would choose him again."

I was suddenly envious of Mom, for being satisfied with simplicity. I was always striving for greatness, for something better than. I wanted to impact the world; she wanted to enjoy her world.

"Maggie, can I share just one more insight to consider?"

I looked at my mom with gratitude. She was treating me with respect, and I suddenly appreciated her guidance. "Yes, Mom, please."

"Adrenaline is intoxicating. It's natural, don't get me wrong, and is wonderfully thrilling; but it can be misguiding as well. A life where you enjoy your every day--that is true living."

We drove on in silence, until she dropped me off at my car. If there was ever an awkward moment in my life with my mom, it was right now. It would have been easy to unlock my car and caravan home with her, but we both knew that I was here to see Peter. "Love you, Mom," I said as I shut her car door.

Mom interrupted quickly, "Choose the life you will enjoy," and she put her hands up in the air to stop any more discussion. That was another moment for her to be stronger than she felt. She winked, and drove off.

I knocked on Peter's door, and he didn't answer for quite some time. I knew he was home, because I could see the glow of a lamp through his window, and so I waited, knocking again. Finally, the door creaked open. Peter had a blanket wrapped around his shoulders, and his hair was disheveled. I had woken him up. I stood there, hesitant at what Peter would do or say, but he assured me that all was well as he slowly pulled me into the apartment and wrapped me into the blanket with him, hugging me with emotion that he had not fully given to me before. I finally broke the embrace.

"You okay?" I asked, as I noticed his eyes glistening with tears. While waiting for his answer, I placed his research backpack on the hallway floor, glad to have it in the safety of his possession.

"I've been playing roulette with my life, skipping my pills like that. Mira gave me a firm tongue-lashing. And Dr. James, well, he told me that I'm lucky to be alive, thanks to you."

"Dr. James actually said something nice about me?" I felt I couldn't show my face in the hospital after the lecture I received from him.

"I was going to sites 7 and 8, alone. I would have died."

"Again," I was quick to point out.

"Again. Yes, die, again," he shook his head in disbelief. "Who are you, my guardian angel?"

I chuckled at the irony of that. "No angel. I'm lost. I don't know anything, except how terrified I was, watching you helpless."

And then it happened. Peter kissed me. It wasn't calculated or planned, or even gentle and soft. It was a kiss that was loaded with zing, energy from all the emotions we were both feeling, passionate and strong.

When we pulled away, Peter smiled, and my heart about exploded. At this moment, I knew my choice, the choice Mom and I had discussed. I was choosing Peter. "I spoke with your father," Peter looked at me, serious yet concerned.

This is not what I wanted to discuss. I wanted to discuss us, and our future. I rushed to explain, "You should know that my dad had a daughter at

204

nineteen and she sort of ran into the arms of lots of men, and I'm sort of his second-chance kid, and he's got issues with me leaving--but I'm not her."

Peter put his finger on my lips to stop me. "He told me to take good care of you."

My jaw must have dropped. My breathing became thick. There was nothing to fight for, nothing to prove to anyone. It all came down to one question. I suddenly became very bashful. "He approves?" I looked at him, knowing that he had control of our future.

Peter walked me to his bedroom, sitting me down next to him, and enwrapped me alone in his blanket. "I see myself out there, with the wolves." He took his hand, brushed my dark hair out of my eyes, and placed his hand on my cheek. "I see myself in a cave, cooking over a warm fire, living free from distraction," he said, just inches from my face, "with someone." My heart was out of control.

"Someone?"

"Don't you see, M? Don't you see, or can you not see what will happen?"

"What?" I asked, confused. "What will happen?"

"I'm not taking you with me." Peter's stare pierced me, and I could hear the hurt in his voice.

"I don't get it." I was dumbfounded.

"You will, one day," Peter said, coolly.

"Is this because I'm young? I am not naïve. I have thought this through--I have calculated every cost and benefit. I'm choosing you, the research, the cave, everything."

He stood up, and walked into the kitchen and grabbed a beer out of the fridge. I felt the short distance he created left a void in our conversation.

"Peter, don't run away, again." I was pulling at strings, trying to make him come back to what we shared moments ago.

Peter offered me some water, and I declined. "Your father told me about Lenora."

"My dad!" I was so confused, not sure if I was sad, or angry, or just plain desperate.

Peter smiled at me. "I'm not taking you." He looked at me and confessed, "Your age is not the problem."

I realized at that moment that I was refusing to hear what Peter was saying. After we sat in silence, I found my car keys and knew what was left to do.

I headed to his front door and noticed his backpack sitting on the floor. As I was about to leave, I turned to Peter and looked him straight in the eyes. "I love you and I know you love me."

Peter nodded, and watched me leave. As I was about to turn the corner in the dark, he called after me, "M, you think I'm strong, but I'm not."

I turned to look at him, wondering what he was referring to.

Peter walked up behind me, confessing, "The night of the accident, I was going on my first date in three years, my first date since Maya left me. A blind date."

I didn't understand why he was telling me this. The thought of Peter with anyone else right now was hurtful. I couldn't hide the tears streaking down both my cheeks. Peter turned me toward him and put both his hands on my shoulders. "I knew I should move on, but I just wanted Maya. We loved each other, but love wasn't enough. I resented this blind date, because it wasn't her. I was just off the mountain and was out of shaving cream." Peter looked straight in my eyes, beyond me to a distant memory. "I saw the car coming. I looked the other way, hoping it would end quickly. I am not as strong as you think I am."

I stood like a statue, not able to move, but he didn't let go until I put my arms around him and finally succumbed to what he was finalizing upon us, which was a farewell. I cried in his arms, the man I felt called to, who was telling me that love isn't enough. After I stopped crying, I whispered in his ear, "You are an idiot. A big, fat idiot."

Peter smiled at me, knowing I didn't mean it but that it would help me to move on. He put his arms around my neck, pulling back to look at me one final time. "I'm an idiot for saying goodbye to you, because I love you. But right now, I'm being strong." He kissed my forehead, and then let go.

"Tell me what it means, your research. I want to know what it all means." I turned away, and walked to my car, not looking back.

Chapter Sixteen: Coping

Two weeks had past since I said goodbye to
Peter. Two weeks of working in the shop alongside
Dad, helping customers find their Christmas gifts,
and painfully faking my joy at every love-entranced
couple that we served. Dad seemed content to
have me back, and never mentioned my stint with
the wolf man, as he called him once. Peter said
that I should move on, and I had--if you call
inhaling and exhaling living. I started running
again on Tubbs Hill, alone. I wanted to take the
risk of running on the icy, dark and dangerous
terrain in the dead of winter. It became an early-
morning battle that I needed to conquer. In the
evenings I moped around the loft and drowned
myself in *Gone with the Wind,* an all-time favorite
that seemed especially appropriate for some
reason. I had a list of classic novels that end
tragically, and I figured I'd just keep befriending
them until one of them made me feel somewhat
better.

December in North Idaho is reminiscent of an
old-fashioned holiday card with horse and sleigh.
The hanging poinsettia baskets draped across
street lamps added beauty to downtown Sherman
Avenue. When the first snow hit in mid-
December, everyone commented on what a
picturesque, magical downtown we lived amidst,

with the white lights draped on every tree, the resort decked out with whimsical lights and festive displays, and the beauty of the lake and the mountains in the background. I just smiled and gritted my teeth, feeling anything but nostalgia this winter. My heart was empty, and my future completely devoid of hope.

A layer of fresh, glistening snow covered the streets the morning Julie came into the shop, along with her now-steady boyfriend, Corbin. Julie was on holiday break and often stopped in after spending time at the coffee shop next door. She looked at me with forlorn eyes, but I didn't want to accept her sympathies, even though I had shared with her my heartache.

"Hi, Mr. Whitaker," Julie announced, as she plopped a bagged scone and orange juice down in front of me. "Compliments of Henry. Says you need fiber." Julie confidently walked in and approached Dad. "Is now a good time to pick up the key?"

Dad looked up with a soft smile, and then nodded.

"Key? Are you working here?" I asked, feeling uncomfortable for being the last to know. Dad shared everything with me that had to do with the shop. It wasn't unusual to hire extra help for the holidays, but I'm surprised neither one of them told me.

"Actually, Corbin is moving in to Donny's place for the holiday. And I'm moving in with you." Julie shrugged a sweet *isn't-this-fun* look at me.

"What? Did I miss the memo?" I was halfway ticked, halfway excited. Julie was the roommate I always wanted yet never had.

"Just for the holidays. Corbin's parents are traveling in Europe, so he has nowhere to go for winter break. And you know me; I can't be around my fourteen-year-old sister for more than an hour. It could turn lethal. You are literally saving her life. My mother is so grateful to you."

"You're moving in with me?" I still couldn't believe it.

"It'll be good for you," Dad stated, matter-of-factly.

"But there's no room," I questioned.

"What are you talking about? Your place is at least twelve inches bigger than my dorm room," Julie joked.

"Dad put you up to this, didn't he?" I finally got the bigger picture.

"Actually, your mom did, but I just prayed the night before to the God Almighty to rescue me from killing my sister, and my prayers were answered," Julie admitted. "It was divine intervention, Maggie. We'll have a Christmas to remember." Julie saw my face unchanged. "Don't overthink it."

"I won't overthink it," I mimicked. Actually, I was already starting to warm up to the idea of having my best friend back.

Since Donny's burglary and the realization that he was a meth addict, I found out that he had also dismantled the alarm to another shop on Sherman two nights later and was subsequently arrested by city police. Donny had spent the last twelve days in jail and would be there indefinitely until his trial date, as Dad or Dawn refused to post bail. Wyn had moved back in to the rental, now that Donny and his destructive entourage slowly disappeared, and Dad arranged for Corbin to stay with Wyn just for the holidays.

Julie worked at the shop alongside Dad and me, and Mom kept busy painting and displaying her work for sale for the first time, mostly in the shop and at Christmas bazaars around town. It was a fairly normal winter, despite my overwhelming depression.

My friendship with Julie picked up right where it left off, with her bubbly existence immersing cheer to my more isolated, private self. She grilled me on every detail with Peter, and as painful as it was to recall him, it was somewhat cathartic to vent it all to her. As I recalled the adventure to his wolf sites and the cave he had transformed into a lodge, I remembered how damp and cold the entire experience was, not to mention downright frightening during the emergency.

"That's not the lifestyle you would want, is it?" Julie questioned.

"If you're asking if I want to go out to the mountains right now, in 22-degree snowfall, no. I wouldn't choose it. But if you're asking if I would do it to be with Peter and show him that I want to be with him, yes, I would have chosen it." I knew that I would have gone to the ends of the earth for him.

"You know what? This *Peter-and-the-Wolf* drama is so obvious," Julie suddenly declared. She jumped over the couch, opened my dresser drawer, and flicked a running brassiere at me. I looked at her, as if she was crazy.

"Obvious?" I questioned.

"Anyone can see that you'd be miserable with him. You hate being cold."

"That doesn't matter."

"Yes, it does! Don't you see?" Julie was quizzing me. "No, you don't see. I can't make you see. Uuughh!" Julie was pulling out her hair, almost frantic. She opened my dresser drawer and threw me socks and sweatpants. I could tell something was brewing in her mind, a plan of some sort. "I know you've been running in the mornings, because I can hear you sneak out. I challenge you to a moonlight race."

"Couldn't you just have tossed me a sneaker or something," I asked, as I held up my bra.

Julie knows how to get to me, and talking through issues doesn't bring resolution. But hammering it out on the pavement does. We ran, amid the night fog and damp air, along the Centennial Trail, which winds along the still, cold lake. Julie's stride had changed in college, and I could barely keep up with her. Something transformed in her, from the lazy runner in high school who giggled and gossiped on each run we shared, to an intense, power-striding athlete whose only comment was the rhythmic flow of her breathing. It took all I had to keep up with her, and although we were silent, my mind raced through the events of the last four months since she had left for college. She was changing, shedding some of her old habits and growing into her new skin. She was a collegiate athlete and had a boyfriend for whom she had actually stuck around long enough to invest in. I had atrophied into a desperate, fate-riddled child, starved for attention. I questioned my future in the shop, becoming an old maid who never left her home town. I wondered what I was missing out on in life. Looking at the lake, vast and foreboding, I sensed how insignificant I was. If my life was a puzzle, I had wasted time trying to put a piece in that didn't fit. Not only did I have the wrong piece, but I damaged it in the process, and the puzzle would now never be perfect. I may never be happy. Peter may never be happy. I was sick with frustration that I got myself into this mess, that we had even met, and that I let myself fall in love.

"Let's stop for a second," Julie breathed through short gasps. I had not realized that not only was I matching her pace, I was setting a new one. We stopped, and Julie gasped for air as she scolded me, "Why in God's good name are you not running on our team? I mean, I'm in the shape of my life, and I can hardly keep up with you."

"I guess I was getting it out." I smiled, a true smile, for the first time in a while.

"You know what you need?" Julie had something in mind, and it was something only Julie would think of.

"What do I need?" I snickered.

"Fun." Julie bent down and stirred her fingers in a mud puddle, and spread mud across her cheeks in a streak, as Indians on a warpath.

"What are you doing?" I laughed.

She reached down again and gathered more mud, this time streaking it on my face. "Follow me."

We retraced our steps back to town, but this time she led me through neighborhoods until we reached Donny's old rental house.

"Corbin is always freaking me out, and now is the perfect time to get him back." She ducked under the front window to spy on where he was inside. "Come on. You have to help me. I think Wyn's home, too."

Wyn. I hadn't talked to him since I asked him for a ride to Wallace, the exact conversation when I told him that he and Trish didn't have the type of love that Peter and I shared. I'm sure Wyn wasn't going to welcome any pranks from me.

"I'll watch from over here," I said, trying not to be a poor sport. I walked away from the window that Julie was squatting under, and walked around to the back of the house. I could hear Wyn's muffled voice and was curious as to what he was up to. I peaked into the window, which was the backside kitchen window box, and watched as Wyn put his arms around a figure of blonde hair. He gave her a quick nuzzle on the neck and a pat on the butt, and Trish turned toward him as her face lit up with joy.

Pounding and beating on the window startled me out of my voyeurism, followed by Julie's hysterical laugh. I could see Wyn and his girlfriend both startle, wondering who was pounding on their front windows. Julie raced to the front door, and Corbin stood there, applauding her efforts, until his hands went over his heart. She had succeeded. Julie then called for me, and I walked out of the bushes and into the front lawn, giving a polite wave. Wyn and Trish appeared at the door, and I saw Wyn see me, just as we ran away into the darkness.

Julie was laughing at her success, and I felt envy, of Julie, of Corbin, and of Trish.

It was Christmas Eve, and Dad was preparing for one of the busiest days in the shop. I skipped my morning run and went into the back studio early to finish some Lenora pieces. Dad was already melting silver.

"Morning, Dad," I greeted. "You know where I'll be," I announced, as I sipped my OJ and slipped into the studio with my scone.

"You might be interested in this." Dad tossed the morning paper on the counter, and tapped at the Calendar of Events in the Local section. The paper advertised the Idaho Fish and Game public hearing of the Gray Wolf Management Plan with guest field biologist Peter Delano. The purpose: to introduce not only current wolf counts, but also breakthrough research of the North Idaho/Montana wolf packs and their behavior, to be held today at noon in the library conference room.

Peter's research. I hadn't forgotten, yet I didn't feel that I could see him again. Even more, I asked him to share with me what he had found. So far, he had not made any attempt to contact me.

For the next hour, I toyed with the idea of going to the meeting, or staying away from Peter. I doubted I could see him without conjuring up painful feelings. I wish I could take it all back, so I didn't have to feel this way. Being away from him was the only way I knew to cope.

The door bell jingled to the shop, and Dad cheerily offered a "Merry Christmas" to the young fellow who sheepishly found his way to the engagement settings. His hands were shaking.

"What can I do for you today?" Dad offered in his usual jovial manner.

"I'd like to get an engagement ring, today, if possible."

"Christmas Eve engagement. That's the way to do it, son. Timing is everything. Come on down here and we'll take a look at what we have in stock. What's your name, son?"

"Conner."

"Conner," Dad repeats. "Come here, Conner, and see if any of these settings jump out at you." I peered around the corner of the studio and spied Conner. He was looking into the glass intently, examining settings while his eyes searched.

"That one." Conner pointed at a ring, princess cut with a cluster of diamonds to one side.

"An unusual choice," Dad commented. "Tell me about the girl."

"She's an unusual girl." Conner started to blush, his eyes sparkling. "She's different than anyone I've ever met. She's one of those girls who won't wear two of the same earrings. She likes things unbalanced. She's strange, but she's so interesting and she has an opinion about everything. This ring seems off-balanced, but it's strikingly beautiful."

I was listening to everything Conner was revealing, and couldn't resist vocalizing a little history behind Lenora's inspiration. "Beethoven," I said matter-of-factly, "because love is deaf."

Conner cocked his head at me, and smiled, "You mean love is blind?"

"Basically, but in Beethoven's case, deaf. Lenora named this setting Beethoven based on the belief that when you are in love, you mute out all the noise and all the distractions that complicate love, so that all you hear is what sounds pleasing to you. So if something is strange and quirky, you see it as interesting, and you choose to love, even if it isn't all round and perfect and smooth."

Conner looked at the ring, then at my father. "Size six and a half."

"We don't have six and a half today," Dad admitted. "I can loan you a temporary setting until it's sized."

"I'll size it today. Give me two hours," I offered.

Conner smiled and thanked me. Then he asked Dad, "Do you get down on your knees these days?"

"Do what she wants," Dad warned. "Always do what she wants." Dad winked. Conner nodded, and signed the paperwork I slipped to him. "We'll work out the payment arrangements when you pick it up."

Conner left, and Dad followed me back to the shop where I had two pendants to cast and a ring to solder together before noon, and a special-order Lenora band to cast by five. "What are you thinking, Margaret? We can't offer same-day service on the busiest day of the week."

"He was the one, Dad. He was the one whom I designed Beethoven for. It's Christmas Eve, and he shouldn't propose with an imposter."

"Who's going to work the front office?" I gave him my pleading eyes, and Dad resigned, "You are becoming more like your mother every day."

I picked up the phone and called Julie. She was living rent-free and could cover the front just until Dad finished his soldering.

"You know, Dad, I think Beethoven would have given up his genius to have his hearing back."

"You think? Why do you say that?"

"He lost his hearing. He knew what his gift was. And he lost the ability to enjoy it. If it were me, I would want to hear what I created, not just watch people clapping or see the joy in their faces. I would want to hear it."

"I'm sure he wanted to hear his music. But he felt it. He felt the vibrations."

"It's not the same."

"What choice did he have? He lost his hearing, and he could have stopped playing or just accept what happened and continue to offer the gift."

"What lesson is that?" I was getting mad, feeling my heart break again. "Here is the best gift in the world, and now let's take away your ability to enjoy it, just so people will think you're amazing one day."

"His gift wasn't listening to music. His gift was creating it, playing it. There's joy in sharing your gift, like Lenora does."

What my Dad didn't realize is that Beethoven had a botched concert, a performance where he couldn't perform properly; and after he failed to perform Piano Concerto #5, he never performed again. I did the research when I decided to name the setting after him, because I had always imagined that he was so virtuous to continue to play while deaf. In reality, it became a big struggle and impediment. There wasn't joy in sharing anymore.

And as I worked, using my gift to bring joy and beauty to others for Christmas, I felt joy's absence.

The door jingled and in walked Julie, with Corbin.

"Reporting to duty," she declared. "I figured Corbin could also help, since he's got some rent to pay as well."

"That would be wonderful," Dad responded. "You're just in time to kick this young lady out." Dad looked at me and said, "You've got ten minutes to make it."

"Make what?"

"The wolf hearing."

"Dad, I can't go. I have so much work to do," I said, with nervous fear now rushing through my mind.

"Now that your replacement is here, I can take over in the back. You better hurry."

"Dad!" I insisted. "I can't go. I can't see him. It wouldn't be appropriate."

"It would be very appropriate, since you have been invited."

"I've been invited?"

Dad pulled out a white embossed stationery envelope, with my name personally written on the front envelope. "This was in the mail slot this morning, and I didn't show you because we had so much work to do. Call me selfish. However, I can see that you need to go."

Dad handed me the thick envelope. I pulled out the card, which had a picture of the Panhandle National Forest on it. I opened it, to see Peter's dark ink handwriting.

Dear M,

My private research is complete, and I'm sharing it at the Idaho Fish and Game hearing on Christmas Eve, noon, at the library. I would be honored if you would attend. What we caught on tape that last day is the culmination of three years' study, and without your good judgment to bring the data back, I would have missed out on the evidence I was trying to capture these years. You are a significant part of this research, and a huge part of my life.

*Please attend, if you can. I have much
to share with you.*

*Your friend,
Peter*

What stuck out to me was his closing, *your
friend*. I knew I couldn't be Peter's friend. We had
been through too much together and experienced
too many feelings to be friends. I can survive
without him, but I can't figure out how to be
happy. I did ask to know what his research meant.
He was honoring my request.

I put on my coat, took the letter in hand, and
smiled at Dad, Julie and Corbin. "I'll be an hour."

Chapter Seventeen: The Research

The Coeur d'Alene library was packed with wildlife conservationists, hunters, businessmen, and the common sort of North Idaho outdoorsmen, so much that I sat in overflow seating behind a broad-shouldered man in camouflage and a baseball cap. This offered some relief as I was more than hopeful to be anonymous during the hearing. Peter was in dress pants and a pressed shirt, looking more put together than I had ever seen him. My head raced with anxious thoughts, and I questioned whether my heart or my breathing was making too much noise.

The city mayor stood up to take the podium, on a slightly elevated stage off the floor, and spoke into a microphone. "Good afternoon, and welcome to the third public hearing of the Gray Wolf Relocation Assessment and Management Committee in conjunction with Idaho Fish and Game's 2009 decision to reclassify the Western gray wolf as threatened, not endangered. This hearing, which is required by federal law to be open to the public, will be recorded and is used to help determine our state's position on the stability of the Northern Rockies gray wolf, its success in our state, and positions to take in the future regarding management of the gray wolf population. To begin this hearing, I would like to introduce the

Idaho Fish and Game's State Wildlife Game Manager."

A burly man of about fifty yelled among the masses, "The wolves are destroying our elk, our deer. Are you going to address that?"

"And my cattle," another chimed. Murmuring and guffawing started to rumble throughout the room, and it was obvious the crowd was not going to be passive.

A thin, older gentleman sitting next to Peter in the front row arose, and took the podium as the mayor sat down. "Good morning, and happy Christmas Eve, happy holidays, Hanukkah, and greetings of all kinds. I know in Idaho how *sensitive* we are as a people, and please know that I mean no offense when I offer all faiths a very happy holidays."

"And in that regard, one of the foremost sensitive issues in our region is our focus today, that being the reintroduction of the canis lupis, or gray wolf. Formerly extinct in our state and primarily extinct in almost the entire United States, great effort, amidst great controversy, was made to reintroduce the wolf in 1994 to Central Idaho, Montana and Wyoming. The multiple layers of controversy have been duly noted when re-establishing the wolves, and as part of our efforts to ensure an effective reintroduction, we organized an Assessment and Management Committee. The wolf brings balance to our ecosystem, naturally stabilizing the overgrowth in populations of elk, deer, moose and coyote, strengthening their breeds as a whole."

"Bullshit!" was yelled from among the group of hunters. "Balance? Overrampant predation! Tell it like it is!"

"I beg for your respect, patience and tolerance," the wildlife game manager warned. "And may I assure you, the Fish and Game works for you, the people of Idaho. We are interested in and respect your views, opinions and concerns. We do not represent the interests of the wolves, but are citizens among you who want to make the right decisions for our state. Idaho is a prohunting state, may I assure you. But I must ask everyone here to save their comments for the end, with civility, and at that time we will field questions." He took a long pause, scanning the room to assess the dynamics present at the hearing.

"The wolf, being top predator, has successfully multiplied breeding pairs, and is thriving today throughout Idaho, Montana, Wyoming, Western Washington, and even Oregon. In the fall of 2005, the population of wolves in Idaho exceeded our predictions of reproduction and surpassed our required breeding pairs of 796, and therefore was taken off the endangered species list. The population has increased even further, and last fall by a vote of 3-2, Idaho offered wolf tags for hunting, capping the harvest limit to 157 in Region 8 of which you live. Since then, petitions to put wolves back on the endangered species list have been submitted to IFG from area conservation groups, and since the population of wolves has stopped growing at such an alarming rate, we must consider why."

"Who cares about the wolves!" One angry citizen yelled out from the middle of the room. "They are destroying our availability to hunt elk and feed our families!"

"They're threatening my cattle! Ninety percent of my pregnant females miscarried last fall after being spooked by wolves."

"The government doesn't reimburse miscarriages," another man interjected and raised his fist.

"I understand that, and let me reiterate that during this hearing, we respectfully remind you that we will be addressing all those issues and taking comments at the end."

"Fish and Game has their own thwarted agenda," yelled an angry man as he stood up.

"Please remain seated and listen respectfully to what the research shows us today." I noticed four police officers enter the back door of the room, making their presence. I was starting to understand the need for Peter's hideout in the woods and his privacy in Wallace.

"The Gray Wolf Relocation Assessment and Management Committee has looked at every possible angle of the wolf controversy and gave their recommendation for controlled hunting in 2009. That was year one of hunting, and we offered 220 wolf tags, charging Idaho residents very little, but out-of-state hunters a substantial fee, bringing into the state 1.2 million dollars in revenues. There were only 56 wolves harvested, far under the limit, and yet when I say 56 wolves, we do our best to determine if they are alphas, betas, male or female, yearlings, lone wolfs, etc. The harvesting of wolves, and more specifically which ones in a pack, will alter the future populations. Through the assistance of a federal grant, Idaho was able to hire field biologist Peter Delano to study the populations in Region 8 for the last ten years. To report his findings, please join me in welcoming Field Biologist Peter Delano."

Peter stood up, and the public remained silent, the tension thick in the room. He walked slowly to the podium, adjusted the microphone to his face, arranged his notes, and then lost his balance slightly. He held on to the podium for stabilization, possibly support.

"Good afternoon. I think it is important for you to know why I was hired, and what I have been doing for the past ten years. I live in two locations: a small apartment among the people, and a camp in the mountains among the wolves. I was hired to study them, watch them, count them, collar them, know them, and report my findings. I was not hired to give opinions, tell the state what to do, or how to manage the wolves. I simply present the research--the unbiased data. Now, have I made opinions along the way? Sure, I have. It's impossible not to. But I have made every attempt to conduct my research and my findings with ethics, with unfiltered, raw data presenting its bias alone. To further explain to you the research that I have been conducting, along with the data that I have acquired, I have a PowerPoint presentation to help you visualize what is out there. Most of you will never see a gray wolf. They are very elusive. The numbers from this first year's low harvesting rate supports that fact. But they're out there, and yes, they are thriving."

Peter turned on the projector, and someone dimmed the lights as the picture of site 8 was projected, his camera box set up in the field. "I have been studying the wolves on the Idaho-Montana border and have been tracking a pack of eight wolves in the Clearwater Range who have an approximate 50-mile territory. I chose this pack primarily because they have a smaller territory, and I have somewhat easier access to them. I set up three sites where I can videotape them, and I weekly check the footage to count their numbers, observe their behavior, and study their survival. I started working with the wolves in the year 2002 by helping Fish and Game tag wolves and pinpoint pack territories throughout the region."

"Five years ago, I chose this pack to study. They are an average pack. They are stable, and hunting takes place in this area." He advanced the slide, which showed video footage of the wolves walking in front of the camera, numbering seven. "In 2007, only seven wolves were discovered on camera. Upon further investigation, indeed, a hunter from Montana harvested wolf #25, a beta male. In the spring, there were only six wolves in the pack, as noted on this next slide. Wolf #22 was missing, a beta female. No tag was claimed for her, so there are a couple conclusions: She could have been kicked out by the alpha female, she could have been poached, or she may have fallen ill or been killed by another animal. Regardless, she is no longer with this pack, and yet you will notice that this wolf here in the back is somewhat bulky. She is the alpha female, and carrying her spring litter of 7 wolf pups, which she delivered sometime in May. So the pack went from six to thirteen, after the birth of the pups. Four of the pups did not survive. Distemper ran through the area, and only three survived. So the pack is now at nine, approximately where it started."

Peter looked up at the room before advancing the PowerPoint image. "Balance seems to be the root word when discussing the gray wolf. Does restoring the gray wolf to our area restore all animal life's natural balance? Does wolf predation balance the overgrowth of elk and deer we have seen in years past? Do diseases such as parvo and distemper balance out the overgrowth of the wolf? Or does the wolf presence, which has caused the area's elk and deer to flee deeper into the mountain ranges, cause the wolves to now search for new food sources, including wide-open ranges that house area ranchers' prized cattle? Yes, wolf attacks on cattle ranches are reimbursable, but I am aware of the heightened miscarriages occurring when a herd is spooked by the attack, and no, miscarriages are not reimbursable."

"So, in effect, the question is, is the wolf creating balance, or wreaking havoc? What does the science show?" Peter advanced an image to show a graph, dating back to 1994 when the wolves were introduced, with sharp inclines in red, until it flat-lines in years 2008, 2009, 2010 and 2011. "You can see in this graph that clearly the wolves have increased in population since '94, but in the last four years, they have stabilized. They have found their equilibrium, even among hunting, which began in 2009. Second question is, are they providing other wildlife stabilization, or is their predation wreaking havoc? Well, we can count the numbers of elk, moose, deer, and see that they have decreased since '94, yet their numbers have stabilized too. It has been claimed that wolves only hunt the weak, sick, young or old ungulates-- hoofed animals. They cause their prey to become stronger, more defensible, and only the weak are taken. This certainly seems like a way that nature balances itself out."

Peter then paused, looked at the footage, and lifted up a remote-control pointer. He advanced the PowerPoint to show a picture of a wolf with a bloodied muzzle. "This here is your Northern Rockies gray wolf, a powerful predator. Are there anomalies in nature? Sure. Are there anomalies in wolf packs? Sure. Wolves are family, but they fight. They kick one another out. Not only do they have rivals with other wolf packs, they can kill each other when provoked." Peter paused, looking at the wolf in awe. "This infighting may provide natural balance of the packs. When a pack grows too large for its territory, some wolves may need to leave. It's all part of balance."

"I know that many of you in this room want to preserve the wolf, as you can see its beauty and power. Hunting for sport seems wrong, unnatural. Some of you want the wolves relisted as endangered or fear they will become endangered with continued hunting. According to these results, the numbers show their populations are stable. With rampant, noncontrolled hunting, yes, they could become endangered. In children's books in every library across America, you will find picture books on the gray wolf and their incredible gift to nature, their predation of the weak, their kills being food for all the lesser animals such as bald eagles, ravens, coyotes. But what you won't find in those often overly cheery books is the fact that wolves enjoy hunting, not unlike man, sometimes just for the thrill of the chase. What I'm talking about is what I've spent ten years hoping to capture on film, something that I knew was happening, but couldn't prove until now."

Peter pushed a button on his remote and video started to play--a pack of wolves, bloodied, lying near their latest deer kill, when a white-tailed deer crosses the camera. At its heels are two young yearlings, snapping at the hindquarters of the deer until it stumbles in the river, falling just before exiting the other side. One wolf chomps the jugular and ends it all. All caught on tape.

"A double kill. These wolves do not need this deer. They are not planning to eat it," as the video shows one wolf walk away, crossing the river again, joining the pack. The other wanders into the woods, near the cave that Peter and I stayed in. "Unlike what you have been told about wolves, they take more than they need, at times. They love to hunt, sometimes for sport."

"Again, in your library books on wolves, you will read that wolves are no threat to man. Let me remind you that wolves and man have not met in a hundred years. Wolves don't know you exist. And yes, wolves prefer ungulates. But wolves will kill, just to kill, for the love of the hunt. They will act like happy dogs, wagging their tails, sitting and seeming to respect your space."

Peter again pointed his remote to the screen, where he had a still of me, face-to-face with the gray wolf. "As cute as a Siberian Husky, make no mistake: This wolf is studying this girl, learning about her, detecting her movements, and potentially preparing to attack. If this wolf had not just tired and filled itself with *two* kills previously, it is possible that she may have been his next victim. Wolves have no fear of predators, until this hunting season. Wolves now have a new predator: man. And man now has a predator, the canis lupis. We have released a shark into the woods, a beautiful, strong predator, which kills, for fun."

"I have seen alphas killed, betas killed, packs reduced by disease, but I have not seen a region wiped out of wolves yet, not since our reintroduction in '94. They have proven to be extremely resilient."

"Balance can be understood and hopefully achieved when studying disorder. When you have disorder, you have to insert energy to reestablish order. What is the energy needed when regulating wolves to maintain a state of order in Idaho? That is for Fish and Game to determine. Using the research, now seeing that the wolves are evasive, resilient, thriving, and a predator who kills for fun, it is the Fish and Game's obligation to set rules and regulations to create the balance they feel serves you all best. That is what my research shows today, and I thank you for your time. All questions regarding management of the wolves must be directed to the Fish and Game. Thank you."

The room fell silent. Peter took a step back, the image of a powerful gray wolf still projected behind him. He glanced at the audience, his eyes carefully scanning the crowd. The wildlife game manager stepped toward the podium, whispering to Peter as they passed one another. A police officer approached and placed his hand on Peter's back, encouraging a quick escort to the exit as heated questions started firing from the crowd.

"One at a time, please. Yes, you in the back," the President pointed at a tall man in flannel.

"According to the research, the wolf is not in danger or even threatened. Will you consider extending the hunting season through spring, and how do you plan to compensate ranchers for spooked cattle?"

230

I did not hear the rest of his question, as I quickly skirted out of the meeting, wanting to catch Peter before he left. Outside the library were two security cars and a media car, and Peter walked with the officer to the parking lot. I ran to him, calling "Peter! Peter!" when an arm caught my own from behind, burning my skin as it tightened around my bicep.

"Miss, questions are being fielded in the room only," the officer said while grabbing me.

"I know him. We're friends."

"Sure, well, I'm real sorry, Miss," He said, almost condescendingly.

"M?" Peter voiced, and walked toward me, leaving a security officer to wait in the parking lot. "I know her. She's safe," Peter explained to the officer. "Just give us a minute."

I looked at the officer as if to say, *I told you so* as he stepped away. "What's with the escort?" I asked.

"You would think it a bit excessive, but it's very real."

"I'm starting to get a sense," I admitted. "That picture of me, it's wrong."

Peter looked quizzical, "Why do you say that?"

"That wolf wasn't going to hurt me. I could feel it."

"You can't trust everything you feel now, can you?" Peter quipped immediately.

"Instinct is natural, biological." I was going to fight for my right to not be made a fool. "I knew he wouldn't hurt me, and he didn't."

"Knowledge is part of the picture, M. Instinct is a powerful tool, but combined with knowledge and experience, it's much more accurate. Our instinct is to not touch fire, but until you've been truly burned, you really don't know why. And don't we all disregard our instincts, sometimes?"

"I guess I was pretty dumb, huh?" I felt weak and embarrassed.

"We both had our lapses in judgment," Peter acknowledged. "I should have never gone to the field just out of the hospital, and I knew it." He looked at me sadly, "I should never have taken you."

Peter saw the disappointment in my face, and it stung to hear that I was a mistake. "Your place is in the shop, Margaret. You were designed to create. It's your gift and your passion. It's not mine. Mine's up there." He turned to look toward the hills.

"Tell me one thing," I was staring at him, forcing my final confrontation. "How do you get over heartache?"

Peter reached for me and pulled me to his warm chest, hugging me with a finality that I did not want to accept. "You're stronger than me, M. Just, don't step in front of a car." This made me laugh despite my sadness. "Remember my lecture on disorder and energy. You have to put energy into living the life you want. It doesn't just happen. You have to make it happen, one step at a time."

Peter let me go, kissed my forehead, and then glanced at his watch. "I've got to go, and these officers are here to make sure I make it out of here in one piece."

"What, have you got a date?" I teased, not even considering the possibility.

Peter looked uncomfortable. "Energy. It's Christmas Eve," he shrugged, "why not?"

My heart dropped, as I realized he was dressed up, not only for the hearing but for another woman. "I would tell you to have a great time, but being that I'm seething with jealousy, I will just wish you a Merry Christmas."

Peter smiled, looking at me sweetly, "One step at a time." He held his gaze at me, before whispering, "Merry Christmas." He left me standing there, in the lightly falling Christmas-Eve snow.

I watched him leave, as if in slow motion, and my time with Peter was over almost four months after it started. I looked up at the forces of nature slowly drifting down upon my head, wetting my eyelashes, the flurry of soft snow melting into the ground it met. I turned, viewing all three hundred and sixty degrees of my surroundings: Tubbs Hill, the lake, the resort, the library, with Sherman Avenue shops just beyond my loft. I watched as Peter drove his car away, and the police officers resumed their posts outside the library meeting room filled with opinionated ranchers, hunters, conservationists, and locals who wanted black-and-white answers in a forever gray area. Everyone in that room wanted to make a difference, wanted to know their rights and rally their causes. So many different opinions, no right answers.

I knew what I had to do. I knew that Peter was a gift, a lesson of sorts, a love, but ultimately a teacher. Peter taught me how much I don't know. I know the life I want, but I don't quite know who I am. Energy was going to change that. I am going to know myself. I am going to assert energy to achieve the changes I want.

That night, I celebrated the eve of Christmas with my mother and father at their home in Coeur d'Alene, where I announced to my family that I am hoping to attend university in two weeks, expecting joy and encouragement. This was the night my childhood reality changed, and the adult realizations set in. Dad announced, through soft smiles, that the house was for sale, starting the day after Christmas. He was not prepared for the downturn in the economy to last so long, and he had previously remortgaged the house to keep the shop afloat until the economy improved. Now he was having a tough time making payments.

Realizing my parents were not as set in their future as I had originally assumed, I offered to stay home, in which Mom refused. "You will go to college, Margaret. We'll take out loans." Dad admitted that he had spent my college savings on paying the mortgage when he thought I had chosen not to go, and it had already run out. He insisted that he truly didn't want to retire, that his shop was his life. Mom was going to work with him.

Now that I was preparing to attend college, they were going to live in the loft. I couldn't see my mother, especially, living in the loft. She was so much more sophisticated than that. "You do what it takes, Margaret," she insisted, and always mentioned that they have their health, which is all anyone can ask for anyway. "This is your time now, Margaret. Go, educate yourself, and get away for a while. We've had our time. Don't worry about us."

Those were selfless words, and I was going to take their advice. They had had their time, and now it was mine, but it still stung. I felt so naïve, about love, about life, about reality. Donny was in jail, Mom and Dad were in debt, and I was completely protected from the realities of life. Peter made that clear at the hearing today, the girl who came face-to-face with a wolf. Disorder. Energy. Balance. Gray. That is how I felt. Everything is just gray, and somehow I have to find a little color in it. Like an artist with three colors, I was going to mix thcm, blend them, try new shades, see what I could make and what I like, starting on fresh canvas. Undoubtedly, I'll like the various shades, but I'm sure, every once in a while, I'll long for a little black and white.

Epilogue: Second Chance

It was take two of their first date, and she couldn't believe that she was actually giving this guy a second chance. He had stood her up before, and never emailed to explain anything. In fact, he vanished into thin air, for all she knew. She was used to guys not being interested after one date, but she wasn't used to being stood up. As far as she was concerned, she was not going to ditch her antagonistic personality, as she usually would, since she wanted him to know full well how lucky he was for her second chance, her dour personality and all.

Work for her had been terrible lately. Not only is the setting pretty grim, but her boss had a hold on her that she tried to undo, unsuccessfully. If she could, she would run to the hills and live out in nature, undoubtedly the only place she truly felt free. Everyone knew that was unrealistic, so she tolerated her job, her boss, her existence, hoping and praying that one day she would find a way to get away. She was invited to Christmas Eve dinner with her parents, but eating with her younger, married sister and newborn baby was all too depressing. She chose to eat a quick meal at the cafeteria after her shift ended, and go on this blind date. Get it over with. In fact, her plan was to give him a quick tongue-lashing, down a quick martini, on him of course, and then excuse herself to go to bed.

All that changed when Peter walked into Beverly's Restaurant, on the 8th floor of the Coeur d'Alene Resort, with acoustic live music being sung by a single guitarist. The snow was gently falling over the lake, and when Mira looked up at the man in dress pants and a tucked-in shirt who was a former patient, her stomach nearly flipped. He knew it was her by the martini in her hand, which she told him she would be ordering, and approached the table, offering her white lilies.

"Miriam?" he gawked, yet instinctively pleased.

"Peter?" she blushed. He set the flowers down, next to her. "Thank you, but lilies?"

"I didn't think my blind date would believe me. It was meant as a conversation piece. You see, about four months ago, I was supposed to meet a Miriam at this booth, although I took a detour to the hospital instead."

Mira blushed. She smelled the flowers, knowing that he was forgiven the moment he stepped in the room. "I think I should preface this first date with a few things about myself. I'm cynical, I hate my job, and I especially hate first dates, because people are never as they appear."

Peter laughed, and checked her by saying, "Well, we don't have to consider this a first date, since you've already bathed me and shaved me. And to that cynical girl who hates her job--you're very good at it. You probably just need to spend a little more time with the land of the living."

She liked the sound of his tone. He was as sweet as the day he opened his eyes in the hospital. There was something alive in him. "I'm here, aren't I, with the living?"

Peter looked out the window at Lake Coeur d'Alene, with the snow slowly drifting down, melting into the water. At that, he gave her a toast with his water. "To the living, to life!"

Mira smiled at Peter, knowing that it was time to begin celebrating life, starting the eve of Christmas. "To life!" she raised her glass, truly happy for the first time in a long while.

References:

* Mother Theresa interview came from *Something Beautiful for God*, Malcolm Muggeridge. Harper & Row, Publishers. 1971.

* *Catcher in the Rye*, J.D. Salinger. Little, Brown and Company, Publishers. 1951.

About the Author:

Rachel Karns lives in Coeur d'Alene, Idaho, with her husband Erik
and their three children, Julia, Alex and Andrew. This is her debut novel.

To contact me:

http://rachelkarns.blogspot.com
email: rachelkarns@gmail.com

Special Thanks:

To my first readers, Mom, Erik, Sandy and Shea, thank
you for reading the first draft
and not running away.

To my good friend and scrupulous editor, Sandy, who
is so painstakingly detailed.
You make me better.

To Wendy, for a cover design which absolutely
fulfilled my vision.

To Eva, for miles and miles of listening, rain or shine.

To Julia, Alex & Andrew, for the good life you give
me everyday.

To Erik, for being the one I respect and love dearly.